ONE SINGLE TICKET

ROBERT WALLACE

DEDICATION

To Pam and Cherie, for your support, your unassuming patience, your love and dedication and for putting up with this obsession of ours for over five years, and possibly more years to come.

CONTENTS

Acknowledgments

Prologue   1

1   The Royal Western Hotel   4

2   Dark Forces   12

3   A Locomotive   20

4   The Royal Western Hotel   26

5   Blackfriars Solicitors   36

6   Rigby's Railway Hotel   39

7   Brunel's Drawing Office   41

8   Butter Wouldn't Melt   49

9   A Mystery Face   56

10   Isabelle   61

11   Silent Footsteps   69

12   The Royal Western Hotel   73

13   Light At The End of The Tunnel   82

14   The Dawn Assault   87

15   The Royal Western Hotel   101

16   The Journey To London   108

17   Arbuthnott's retreat In Richmond Hill   114

18   New York City   123

19   New York City   126

20   East 28th Street, New York City   140

21   The Dolphin Hotel, Liverpool   146

Epilogue   150

References   155

Author's Note   156

ACKNOWLEDGMENTS

Researcher: Stuart Amesbury
Editor: Nicky Coates
Designers: Leonard & Bryony Greenwood

Robert Wallace expresses his gratitude to the following people:
Claire Makin – The Tourist Information Centre, Bristol.
Laura Hilton – The Clifton Bridge Trust.
The SS Great Britain Trust and Archive.
Steve Yabsley – BBC Radio Bristol.
Professor Angus Buchanan – University of Bath.
The Steam Museum – GWR, Swindon.
The Bristol Records Office at 'B' Bond Warehouse.
Richard Marshall – GWR Locos 1848 - Laluciole.net
John Lobb, Boot makers of London.
My late friend, André Smolinski; for all his encouragement.
Tony Prosser, Andy and Camilla Jefferson, and Melvyn and
Marianne Plum who read various drafts.
The late Nicholas Brimblecombe and his wife Sally for their help
and input.
John and Pascale Penfold – technical and artistic input.
Guy Coldwell – the hand-drawn image of Royal Western Phaeton.
Sam Snape – the best script consultant anywhere and a great friend.
Gerry Brooke – The Bristol Times
David Tokely – designer at The Lavenham Press, Suffolk.
Len Deighton – for relating the Bible quote from 'Hebrews'.

PROLOGUE

The SS Great Britain, 24th August 1852.

Harry Brooke is sitting out on the weather deck towards the stern of the ship; it's been three days since it left Liverpool. He would appear to be a troubled individual, ashen-faced and maybe feeling just a little seasick. The Irish Sea and the Atlantic swell have not helped matters as the ship heaves, pitches and rolls; the sails crack, flap and complain under the relentless beating they receive. For these are not sheltered coastal waters any longer. The thrum and pulse of the ship's steam engine is steady and constant, driving the propeller, and the ship, on. All the while, the open sea makes its presence known to the uninitiated.

Despite the wind, the deck is being used by a variety of passengers; the air here is decidedly better, and the cramped conditions below become intolerable for long periods, even in a First Class cabin. Whilst attempting to take shelter from the wind,

Brooke removes a roll of paper from his coat pocket, unfurls it and studies it. In contemplation he is grim, and his thoughts are dark.

A lady of a mature, matronly appearance approaches him; he discreetly re-pockets the paper. She would be many years his senior, he thought. She wraps a cloak tightly about herself. Brooke casually thinks to himself that it might be some kind of uniform and her somewhat awkward approach inwardly amuses him, momentarily lifting his dark mood.

She attempts conversation, her voice battling against the wind. "I noticed that you were sitting alone. You seemed a little uneasy and the sea is particularly rough today, are you quite all right, sir?"

Harry had muttered an agreement when she spoke of the sea and the wind.

"Unfortunately, my husband is in the sick bay, and I felt the need of some fresh air." She was plainly trying to make polite conversation.

"Please," he stands courteously, "it is most certainly fresher here, even braving the elements."

He draws a deck chair nearer to his, so she might sit comfortably and they can converse.

"Thank you," she rearranges herself busily and makes a further attempt to engage him in conversation, "I take it you are emigrating, as we and most on board are; if not for the gold, for a new life."

"I don't know about that, I'm not really sure," Harry is vague, possibly an attempt at avoidance. His mouth is dry as he speaks further, "I have recently been working for Mr. Brunel, the man who built this ship."

"I am aware of the identity of the man who built this ship," she says haughtily, "and now?"

Harry takes a breath: "To be honest, I am not sure. I have had two meetings with the Captain about opportunities on board the ship."

"How intriguing, most intriguing." This time she sounds interested and eager to learn more. Is there a suggestion – in the tone of her voice – that she knew something? Or is it his overly speculative imagination once again?

He feigns a smile: "Harry Brooke," he says in introduction, holding out his hand, "and, I am quite well, but thank you for asking."

Her handshake is surprisingly firm, her manner confident, "And I am Mrs. Mary ...."

At that critical moment of introduction, the ropes and canvas scream and yawn, Brooke doesn't catch her surname, he is barely paying attention anyway but she continues unabated. "So, will you return, Mr. Brooke? To England, I mean?"

"I'm not sure;" he turns towards her, sensing her sincerity, and proceeds in serious tones, guardedly, "so much has happened in recent times, some things I might have prevented, maybe I can reconcile those events? A man has died; a close friend - we were working together at the time and I allowed him to be killed by a deluded madman. It was something that should never have happened. But I had also fallen in love, and maybe such affairs of the heart had impaired my judgment? I am not so easily given to such matters. And, even this, gone - I have lost this one opportunity; the only woman I could ever have fallen in love with - lost forever. It's all gone!"

"My goodness, Mr. Brooke! Is this something you would wish to talk about?"

"Maybe," still stony-faced and thoughtful about the words he chooses to use, "you see, I have encountered some truly ruthless individuals who would stop at nothing in their mission to do harm to the success of Mr. Brunel and his investors; to undermine his enterprise, and in so doing destroy one truly revolutionary idea - that of transatlantic steamship travel from London to New York with the purchase of one single ticket. And, that was how I became involved."

"It appears you've had a very difficult time Mr. Brooke. I'm a very good listener, if you do want to talk ...." she doesn't finish the sentence, leaving the idea hanging, but reinforces it, "In my chosen vocation, I have heard the confessions of many; of those previously unknown to me, when there was no available priest. I have spent a great deal of my time in hospitals - in military hospitals, and I can assure you that in those places, this is often a greater requirement than tending to the sick, the wounded and the dying."

"I thought that might be so," he says. "I too have experienced and witnessed the aftermath of bloody battle myself," a comment that is something of an understatement.

Mindlessly, he looks out from the developing conversation, possibly to a far-off place, somewhere beyond the distant horizon, and wonders. Is this now the time? The time to unburden himself of the torment, the anguish and the guilt that has been fermenting inside throughout these last four months...?

1 THE ROYAL WESTERN HOTEL

Bristol – four months earlier

It was an elegant suite of private rooms in the Royal Western Hotel - Brunel used this as his private residence when he was spending time in Bristol. The hotel was situated close to the cathedral, not far from the floating harbour, or from the Great Western Dockyard for that matter. Brunel was in Bristol, his niece was in attendance.

Brunel was always a hive of energy, full of enthusiasm, passion and ambition. He was unique amongst men in his innate ability to grasp the concept behind engineering principles. On this day he was pacing around the lounge, acutely preoccupied. He was wearing his customary attire: a tailed coat and a carefully-knotted silk tie. Slightly more diminutive in reality than one might have expected, but a giant amongst his contemporaries, the 'Chief' appeared almost naked without his trademark stovepipe top hat. His eyes were intense, always focused on something, even if it were cerebral in its nature. His hair, dark and curly with distinguished sideburns, framed a quizzical, cautious countenance. Today he was particularly agitated by something. Everything indicated that he was wrestling with a grievous problem, for all was not well within the world of Brunel or the Great Western Railway Company.

His niece Isabelle, visiting from France, was sitting at the pianoforte, playing Beethoven's Moonlight Sonata, a recital rehearsal piece. She had grown into a very attractive young lady, certainly no longer a child. Isabelle had been blessed with flawless features, and a teasing smile was never far away. She was of slender build and youthfully exuberant. She might have been merely a student of music, but she stood apart. Her dress was decidedly haute couture and was without doubt from Paris. Utterly flattering, it emphasized a palpably nubile femininity. The garment was trimmed with lace from Valenciennes, contrasting with her dark wavy hair, which fell in tresses about her shoulders as she played a crescendo of notes.

Isabelle watched her uncle as he looked through an old sea chest, his temper escalating as he slammed each drawer back into place. He was searching for something, but in vain. To goad him, or just being playful, she played just a little louder. Ultimately, it became a competition of wills between the two of them; finally, he'd had enough.

"Isabelle! Will you please stop tinkering! I am trying to concentrate."

She played a discordant note and looked at him with a coquettish smile.

"What is the matter, Oncle?" She stopped playing.

"I have mislaid some documents. Damn it!"

She resumed her playing, pianissimo now with no real melody, a random series of notes and scales. He glanced at her sideways, all too aware that she was doing this deliberately to exacerbate his bad mood. Such imperfection, even in music, offended him greatly in his desire for perfection in all things.

"They were in this chest … Isabelle, please!"

"But, I have to practice," she insisted. She didn't really mean it and knew that he knew that.

"Yes," he said firmly, "at the music school. That is the place to practice, not now, not here - enchanting as your playing might be."

"NON!" her voice was raised, very slightly, in gentle protest, "It is there that I study; and, if I am to pass my exams to enter the Conservatoire de Paris..."

Brunel chose to ignore her comment, as she knew he would.

"They were in here, I know. I placed them there myself - less than one week ago."

"I am not to blame for this!" she said in mocking, child-like denial.

Brunel strode across the room to the door of the lounge, throwing it open with gusto, calling out into the cavernous, marble-tiled hallway beyond:

"Mrs. M! Mrs. M!" his voice echoed.

His call was responded to by an attractive woman of a certain age; formal and perfunctory, with more than a hint of the Scottish Highlands about her voice.

Mrs. McCready, the senior housekeeper, always announced her presence with a rapid tattoo upon the door, four distinctive taps, and no exception now either.

"You called, sir." it was more of a statement than a question.

"Do we have news of Mr Guppy yet? His arrival plans?"

"Mr Pillinger is collecting Mr Guppy from the railway station as we speak, sir."

Brunel continued to rattle through the chest angrily. Mrs. M approached her voice full of concern.

"Is something wrong, sir?"

"NO! ISABELLE PLEASE!" he raised his voice with displeasure, "Mr Guppy arrives directly. And we have urgent matters to discuss."

Isabelle stopped playing again, with another discord. "Oh! Then I must cease, if you have urgent matters." Those last two words were loaded with playfully accentuated sarcasm. Mrs. McCready shook her head in dismay at the predicament. To her, their occasional quasi-father-and-daughter relationship was a mystery which truly baffled her.

The sound of iron-shod hooves upon cobbles was muted, but distinct enough, and was followed a moment later by a solid knock at the front door.

"Pillinger has returned as expected, sir. If you'll excuse me, and if you are sure there is nothing wrong?" She raised her eyebrows, turning to leave the lounge. Isabelle smiled, as did Brunel; a private joke.

Outside, greetings were being exchanged, the clamour of the horses and the chinking of the leather harnesses more audible now - the carriage door clattered shut. Mrs. McCready called her thanks to the coachman, returning to the lounge with the distinguished visitor.

"Mr Guppy, sir, Miss Louiseau," she announced with an air of gracious formality.

"AHA! My dear friend!" effused Brunel, "Come in, come in. Welcome home to Bristol! Come in. Will you take some refreshment?"

They shook hands, obviously very pleased to see each other once again.

"Good day to you, Chief, and bonjour to you too, Mademoiselle Isabelle! Comment allez vous?"

Isabelle arose from her piano stool, walked towards Guppy sedately, exuding silent charm. Guppy, despite his years, was transfixed as she moved towards him.

"Je vais bien merci, Monsieur Guppy," her tone coy, her accent pronounced, "et vous?"

Mrs. McCready interjected with an air of authority, patently aware of the game Isabelle was playing and of the effect she was having upon the older man: "Come along Isabelle, let your uncle and Mr Guppy conduct their business in some peace. Mr Guppy has travelled a great distance to be with your uncle."

"Urgent matters?" she asked her uncle with a haughty smile.

"OUI, MADEMOISELLE, urgent matters," responded Brunel, without missing a beat.

Thomas Guppy was a mild-mannered man, quietly spoken, genteel and unassuming. He wore a stiff-collared shirt and necktie beneath his dark blue suit. His eyes were blue, his skin slightly pale, his hair and moustache bushy and grey. In truth, he did not look in the best of health, despite his convalescence in the Mediterranean sunshine. He settled in an armchair, making himself comfortable.

"I'll fetch some coffee," said Mrs. McCready. The two women withdrew from the room without further discourse.

"The child can be tiresome, Guppy." shrugged Brunel.

Guppy laughed aloud, looking squarely at Brunel. "She's hardly a child any longer, Chief. What age is she now ... twenty-two, twenty-three? She's a young woman and a very striking one at that. In fact, I'd say she is quite beautiful - do you not see that?"

"No, I cannot!" said Brunel with good humour.

"Ah, you don't mean that, Isambard, I know you only too well. And besides, I know you truly think the world of her, as she does of you. She is good company for you, here in Bristol, whilst you are away from the family in London."

"Maybe." Brunel was casual, but his friend was determined to have the final word.

"Maybe? You know she now lights up any room she enters, and I can see your pride. It is clear. She is both charming as a person and gifted as a musician: you are a lucky man indeed. The rapport she enjoys with you is more profound than that which she shares with her own father. Of that, I am quite sure." Brunel smiled and lit a cigar. "Thank you, Guppy, I am quite aware of the attention she attracts both here and in London. And I can't abide to think what it might be like in Paris, or at her home in Normandy. Finding her a suitable husband - now that seems more of a challenge than building a suspension bridge! She is both demanding and carefree, in equal measure, simultaneously. Our relationship is based upon good humour and mutual respect. Her father, I think, has been too serious with her. He too is an accomplished musician - a violinist. Thank goodness Isabelle has chosen not to follow in his footsteps - that infernal instrument, given her wilful side ...."

It was time to change the subject from familial matchmaking and music to Company business. "How was your journey down from London?"

"Tolerable, although the Swindon break is still far too short and the refreshments available from Rigby's Hotel are a disgrace. Especially their coffee. But, here I am now, fresh and rejuvenated, all the way from Naples."

"Good for you, so glad to hear it. I must say, I am pleased to see you and it does give me the opportunity to personally extend my condolences to you for the loss of your mother, Guppy. She was both elegant and clever, and could teach us both a thing or two whilst we were learning our trade - she was a formidable engineer."

"Thank you, Chief. Inevitably, none can cheat the Grim Reaper. Heaven awaits us all; it's just a question of when that time will come. Ah, but fond memories and a life well lived, as you rightly say. So, you have some news. And, what of our pier scheme and the Company?"

Brunel stood, buying time to formulate his words, wandered to the fireplace and leaned against the mantelpiece. His tone dropped, now he was deadly serious.

"I regret to say that I have very grave news to report, Guppy. My house at Duke Street has been burgled."

"My God! Was ...."

Brunel cut him off, "Yes, I'm afraid our share certificates have been taken. Gone .... yours, mine, Wainwright's, Bellinger's. There is no clue whatsoever as to who might have taken them. But nothing else was removed and there was ample choice - paintings, silverware, things that could so easily have been taken and sold. The thief knew exactly what he wanted and where to find my safe! Which was locked! He even left money kept within the safe - Isabelle's travel allowance."

"I don't know what to say Chief... but how did the thief get in?"

"Of that, I have no idea. There has been no damage, but the situation itself has become desperate. Over time, I have noticed that other things have been moved; various papers, maps, plans."

"Not stolen?"

"No, just moved. It seems that someone has been at work to undermine us, Guppy. I mean to find out who it is and exactly why they would do this."

"I see."

"That's why I had sent word to you, for you to come from Italy. I regret disturbing your convalescence, but it truly is that serious. Furthermore, Nathaniel Bellinger has not been seen for over a month. His family now fears for his wellbeing. They are understandably distraught."

"My goodness, Chief, these matters make my bronchial disorders pale into insignificance! What are we to do? Indeed, what can be done?"

Brunel returned to his armchair beside Guppy's, relieved to have shared this information, yet still agitated by the inconvenience of everything.

"I have sent a message to Cornelius Arbuthnott at Blackfriars."

"Ah yes, of course, but why Cornelius?"

"We require an outsider, an agent if you like, to help us. It has to be a person with no vested interests in our business, other than to investigate on our behalf and, I hope, to solve the problems we face. This individual has to be highly proficient, independent and answerable only to us."

"And has Cornelius identified such a candidate? For his field is surely in patents of scientific and engineering matters, not sleuthing?"

Brunel contemplated these words and wandered back towards the mantelpiece.

"Yes, yes. He has engaged the services of one Harry Brooke; ex 44th British Infantry Regiment, he fought in the Afghan War, some ten years ago. He's thirty-five years of age and, evidently, quite a resourceful chap. He solved that Belgravia diamond theft, scaled the side of some mansion and pursued two armed men, five storeys up, across the rooftops. He collared the thieves and recovered the diamonds. Not bad, eh? Lady Soames says he's a bit of a charmer too ...."

"Aha, yes, that Harry Brooke? I've heard of him. Wasn't he the chap court-martialled for striking a senior officer?"

"Yes, well, that will forever be the record, but what brought him to that action? There are two sides to every story. Besides, Arbuthnott is happy with his choice. He's had Brooke thoroughly vetted. He's meeting him in Paddington tomorrow, to brief him on the task in hand. Brooke will bring a fabricated patent document which we have devised; it is of no true consequence and is based upon Morse's principles for a transatlantic cable, it incorporates a lot of stuff and nonsense!"

"Ingenious, Chief, but will Cornelius be able to convince this Harry Brooke that the documents are genuine, not just a ruse to flush out a spy, and to what end?"

"Yes, I think he will. Cornelius is nothing if not cunning, and that goes hand-in-hand with his specialist knowledge of the law, wouldn't you say? As to the end, I am not sure. But once Mr Brooke takes possession of those documents, he becomes a walking trap. We desperately need to ascertain if this spy is working from here in Bristol, or in London from Blackfriars. Surely it has to be one or the other, does it not?"

"Brooke will know nothing of the break in at Duke Street and the presumed espionage?"

Guppy was beginning to see the broader picture.

"No, not yet, he doesn't need to. He will believe he is merely a

11

courier, delivering secret patent documents, to me personally. But, I have asked Cornelius to suggest that there might be a further errand for which I wish to engage his services, whatever that might be. Neither man will be any the wiser, it's just something else. If he's the man I think he might be, he will be curious about this and, possibly, somewhat flattered that the great Isambard Kingdom Brunel should hire his services." he paused to show he could be joking, a pause which Guppy seemed to appreciate with a wide smile.

"No. Let's get a measure of the man first, let's see if we can trust him. If we are able to do so, we can then bring him into the Company fold, the inner circle, so to speak; only then can we reveal the entirety of our woes. We need to get a measure of the adversary who would oppose us, who he is, and his intentions. I am persuaded by Cornelius that Brooke is the man for this task."

"That, Chief, sounds like a plan as thorough as any you have devised on that drawing board over there."

"Too kind, Guppy, but a plan is what is needed. In the meantime, we'll have to wait and see what might transpire with Harry Brooke, will we not? And waiting is not a favoured pastime of mine."

"No Chief, it most certainly is not," said Guppy with a wry smile, "let's have Pillinger take us up to Clifton. I would very much like to take luncheon at the Club. I can recount my journey to Bristol; it's a devil of a long way from Naples, you know."

"Indeed, Guppy, I'd like to hear all about the journey and your work in Naples. It will be my pleasure to buy you lunch."

2 DARK FORCES

London

Harry Brooke had just enjoyed breakfast in the busy dining room of the Prince of Wales Hotel, in Paddington, West London.

Brooke appeared to be a strongly-built man, blue-eyed and intelligent. Despite his powerful-looking frame, his movements were smooth and economic. Behind this face was a soldier who had suffered many privations: Brooke manifested a complicated blend of contradictions. He was articulate, yet an inherently tough individual. He had drawn a veil over his own self-education and adopted a disposition which masked his origins - the dark cobbled streets near the river; the wharves and docks between Woolwich and Greenwich.

Brooke was adept and skilful, not averse to manual labour; he had learned to cast his own bullets and had carved modifications to the stocks of carbines. He'd been familiar with the pouring of molten iron and the making of steel, of working in the extreme heat of a forge. He was able to appreciate pieces of precision engineering as things of intrinsic beauty, even the machinery and tools themselves. Setting this aside, he had become a man who had accepted certain responsibilities during his life. This, and his facility for decision-making, were duly noted by his senior officers and had enabled his rise through the ranks of the British Army, especially during his service in India. Self-discipline and a sense of purpose had shaped his character, but postings and missions had certainly affected his opinion of military campaigns and what might be achieved in the longer term. The futility he had witnessed in Afghanistan had cemented his cynicism regarding that particular conflict, and of its underlying politics in general.

Brooke was, first and foremost, a survivor, and in order to survive he had relied upon his own instincts for when reacting to such challenges as might confront him. But now, having been discharged from the Queen's service, he had found a new life; and in this incarnation he had become equally at ease dining with clients in Pall Mall as he was exchanging tales with lightermen and bargees on the docks and quays running along the Thames. Such conversations often provided Brooke with very useful information relating to certain cases. He had, so far, managed to survive into his mid-thirties; he had never settled down to a family life, he had neither the time nor the inclination to foster such relationships.

He and his close friend and colleague, Captain Peter Bishop, had been attached to the same regiment in India. They had both fought in the disastrous Afghan campaign of 1842; a military debacle where the British Army had sunk unconquered, yet overwhelmed by the extreme climate, by treachery and subsequent barbarity. They had barely escaped with their lives. That they succeeded in saving the colours was their only degree of triumph.

Officers and enlisted men alike suffered in the brutal bloodshed, the enforced malnutrition, dehydration and - more often - death! During their retreat, on the plain of Kabul and above Gandamak, some four and a half thousand souls had perished. Brooke had been the career soldier. Bishop, his side man, was sagacious, a gifted war artist, deceptively brave in the face of adversity.

Brooke lit a hand-rolled cigarette, engaged it into his favoured ivory holder and picked up a copy of today's edition of The Times. It had been pressed with a hot iron to remove the folds and attached most ingeniously onto a wooden reading frame. He admired the brass clip mechanism with quiet appreciation; it was simple and effective, as such things should be.

The dining room was spacious with a high ceiling, pendant chandeliers, exotic heavy drapes and large sash windows, overlooking Eastbourne Terrace and the entrance to Paddington railway station. The many tables were adorned with starched white linen tablecloths, folded napkins, candelabra and silver cutlery. Uniformed waitresses scurried around busily at the tables, dashing to and from the steaming kitchens.

A bearded man sat at a table beside Brooke; a gentleman in his late fifties sipping from a china cup and studying a letter. A silver monocle was screwed tightly into his eye socket, kept in place by the clenching of his facial muscles around its contours. The absence of breakfast accoutrements suggested that this man wasn't a hotel resident, but probably a guest passing through.

Another man approached Brooke's table somewhat furtively, clutching his hat, slightly breathless. The man, so it would seem, was on a mission. In his other hand he held a leather briefcase which bore some gold lettering, an embossed crest or coat of arms. It suggested some importance or legality. Although the motif was small, it was certainly distinctive.

"Mr Brooke?" the man enquired politely.

Brooke glanced up from his newspaper, feigning surprise; he was clearly expecting someone.

"And you are...?"

The man became uncomfortable, Brooke's tone, the timbre of his voice, bore an air of authority.

"I represent Mr Cornelius Arbuthnott, from Blackfriars' Solicitors. I have a ...."

"And where is Mr Arbuthnott? Brooke consulted a gold pocket watch which he'd withdrawn from his waistcoat with surprising speed.

"He was, uhm, indisposed."

Brooke re-pocketed the timepiece as swiftly as he'd revealed it.

"Indisposed, was he? And, pray tell, with what inconvenience might he be indisposed? Perhaps a horse that's thrown a shoe?"

There was silence, then the man continued. "He merely

15

instructed me to deliver this to you."

The man proffered the briefcase, which Brooke ignored. He held his gaze. "And he offered no message, nor instruction? No proof of identification as is customary in such a transaction?"

"No, sir, none at all."

"That, I am afraid to say, I simply disbelieve. My correspondence with Mr Arbuthnott had persuaded me he was a man of courtesy, of protocol and of reliability."

"Very wise, indeed, sir."

It was the voice of the solitary gentleman from the table beside him, with his screwed-in monocle and worried expression. He continued without turning, his stare fixed ahead, his voice low.

"Caution is a necessity these days, Mr Brooke."

"Now I am confused," said Brooke, just as a lawyer might dismiss unworthy evidence in court, "a possible impostor and his accomplice. Whom might I believe, and why?"

The solitary gentleman stood, turned towards Brooke and bowed slightly.

"I am Cornelius Arbuthnott, Mr Brooke, from Blackfriars, at your service."

He produced some government credentials, which Brooke studied carefully. He waited for a moment. "And where am I bound, Mr Arbuthnott? For only you should know."

"Why, to Bristol, Mr Brooke. To Bristol Terminus, travelling on the Great Western Railway. The train on which you are booked is scheduled to depart at twelve. And what a coincidence it would be if the locomotive was named Courier."

"And then?" persisted Brooke, with a hint of impatience, "What next?"

"Why, but you are to meet the famous engineer, Mr Isambard Kingdom Brunel. He wishes to meet with you, for there are important matters to be discussed. An honour, I do believe."

Brooke smiled, and they shook hands, positions and purpose acknowledged and agreed. Arbuthnott continued: "And, if you can persuade the great man to read and digest the accuracy of these assorted documents and diagrams, you will make my firm extremely content and eternally grateful to you. For Mr Brunel is not generally a man given to bureaucracy, and it's paperwork."

Brooke gestured for Arbuthnott to be seated. "Then take a seat. Will you join me at breakfast?"

"Thank you, no. I breakfasted in my room earlier."

Arbuthnott took the case from the other man, dismissing him without further word. The man acknowledged Brooke with a single nod and the vaguest of smiles, as if to say, well played sir.

Arbuthnott busied himself with the contents of the case as the man turned and left.

"Why all this skulduggery" asked Brooke casually.

"Oh, this is not skulduggery, Mr Brooke. That little piece of theatre was merely a precaution."

"A precaution against what, exactly?"

"I wanted to see just how careful you were; a stranger presents himself, and..."

"Ah, I see. And did I pass your test?"

"With flying colours, Mr Brooke," he lowered his voice to a whisper, "dark forces are at work, even as we speak."

"Dark forces?" Brooke questioned, with a look of disbelief - now this surely was theatre.

"Dark forces are at large, to steal Mr Brunel's revolutionary ideas. Thereby, they would do him harm. It is the world in which we live, I'm afraid. 1852, yet it could be the middle ages."

"Are you serious, Mr Arbuthnott?" knowing full well that he was.

"Why, never more so, Mr Brooke, never more so! Now, we must set about our business. Your train to Bristol departs in less than two hours, and there is much to discuss. It is your understanding of diverse matters that led me to believe that you were the only man for this job. That, and your distinguished military service, of course."

"Yes, although that is now some way behind me, and a little tarnished at that."

"I am satisfied in your defence of a lady's honour and her dignity - from the hands of a boorish husband."

"Yes, who also happened to be my commanding officer."

"But you made the correct decision, Mr Brooke. In any case, a Captain Bishop saved the day for you, as I understand it. And Lady Soames cannot praise your integrity and undoubted abilities highly enough - not scared of heights either, by all accounts?"

Brooke could not help but smile at the recollection: "The diamonds."

"Quite so, and not many would have taken the risks you did to retrieve them. Now, let's go up to my room and I'll show you what all of this is about."

In Arbuthnott's hotel room, a lamp flickered as he sifted through the papers. Brooke found himself a comfortable armchair and waited patiently.

Arbuthnott continued in his somewhat clandestine manner: "Now, the main part of your job is to deliver all of the documents contained in this briefcase to Mr Brunel, personally, in Bristol. I have arranged for you to meet him at his hotel, the Royal Western, not too far from Bristol Terminus railway station. He may have some questions, which you will note, but there is something else, which I will tell you about in a minute. Not that I know very much myself."

Brooke sat back and lit a cigarette, somewhat intrigued: "I see, it all sounds very interesting."

Arbuthnott carefully removed two more pages of complicated technical drawings. Each component of every mechanism was notated. Tiny print detailed the pages. Brooke had never seen anything quite like this before. Similar maybe, but not in such detail and order.

"This is all very much for the future, but it does require Mr Brunel's attention now. These are preliminary patent documents, Mr Brooke, for something of immense importance. So immense that it will change the world in which we live."

Brooke was intrigued: "Documents for what, if I may ask?"

"They describe a unique method, in great technical detail, of exactly how to lay a transatlantic telegraph cable from east to west. A ship will be built especially to accomplish this feat of engineering, requiring specialised cable-laying machinery installed upon the vessel. This has never been attempted before."

Brooke was astounded for, of course, he knew this was unprecedented.

Arbuthnott continued, "This is essentially a line of continual communication which will link Europe with the New World; more aptly, Great Britain with the United States of America. Two thousand, six hundred miles, give or take. The cost will be enormous, as will be the risk. A company will be formed to organise the finance; therefore secrecy is absolutely paramount."

Brooke breathed out a sigh of utter incredulity: "Impossible, surely?"

"No," replied Arbuthnott, "difficult, but possible. Samuel Morse has already produced and established a viable electric telegraph line overland between Washington and Baltimore. It was funded by the U.S. Congress. It is the way of the future; believe me, one day conventional mail will be obsolete."

Brooke was rendered speechless that such a notion was at all possible.

"Needless to say, Mr Brunel and his team in Bristol are very anxious to see these diagrams. With the invention of the screw propeller, the SS Great Britain sails fast and true. The new ship will sail equally straight, but at a much slower speed, in order to lay the cable successfully into such a huge depth of the ocean. Just imagine the sheer weight and of the counter-balances required for such an endeavour. Of course, protection of the cable and insulation from the sea water, are other considerations."

"And this is why the dark forces, as you put it, seek to jeopardise Mr Brunel's plan - or to prevent its success?"

Arbuthnott considered for a moment, approached the window, peering out over Eastbourne Terrace, as if looking for potential saboteurs. He waited for a few long seconds, choosing his words carefully.

"All of this is a long way off, but can you imagine what opportunities lay ahead if we can communicate with America? Commercial and military communications of course, as well as political and maybe even social interactions."

"It sounds unbelievable."

Arbuthnott arched an eyebrow: "No, it is entirely believable. One day ordinary people will communicate across continents and oceans, it has to happen. But for now, your job is to deliver these documents to Bristol. All of this is completely confidential and highly secret."

Arbuthnott paused again, then looked Brooke in the eye. "There is, however, this other matter I mentioned earlier; another errand with which Mr Brunel wishes to engage you, the nature of which I know not. He was most secretive about this, but I know it is something which concerns both him and his colleague, Mr Thomas Guppy, greatly."

"It all sounds most intriguing," said Brooke.

Arbuthnott smiled: "If it involves Mr Brunel, it will be so. Now, the train will not be protected, so you are on your own. I take it you are armed?"

"Yes, indirectly I am, anyway." Brooke removed his pocket watch, "I think it's time."

A porter walked with them out onto Eastbourne Terrace and across to Paddington railway station; he wheeled a large travelling case whilst Brooke clasped the precious briefcase.

Across the road, a man in a dark cape was lighting a pipe. It was a distraction, for he watched the scene with interest and slowly, very slowly, he followed them at a plausible distance.

Meanwhile Arbuthnott said in a lowered voice, away from the porter, "Mr Brunel always has a vision you know, like all great pioneers of the past, and those of the future. This magnificent station, the locomotives, his railway tunnel at Box, the railway terminus at Bristol, the hotel and the steamships down there. But most of all, a journey which starts from here, in Paddington, to Bristol and then directly across the ocean to the New World, on one single ticket."

Brooke now raised his eyebrows. "Incredible, Mr Arbuthnott."

"Please convey my best wishes to Mr Brunel and ensure that he administers those documents. Time, Mr Brooke, is of the essence."

"I will do that for you."

With that, he turned and walked away, across to the other side of the station, towards the ticket offices. Inside that curmudgeonly appearance, Arbuthnott was a cunning bluffer, a secret spymaster and a keeper of secrets; many had underestimated him.

Harry Brooke smiled at the departing figure, he tipped the porter and walked further into the station towards his train, and noticed that the locomotive was indeed called Courier - was that a coincidence? He had his ticket ready as he approached the smoky platform. He saw that his trunk was being loaded into a rear goods carriage.

Behind, the man who had been lighting his pipe moments earlier also descended the ramp and he too held a railway ticket. As the station clock clicked to midday the locomotive jolted, gaining traction and momentum, moving slowly away from the platform with great hisses and through clouds of steam. Both men were now on that westward-bound train.

3 A LOCOMOTIVE

The Great Western Railway

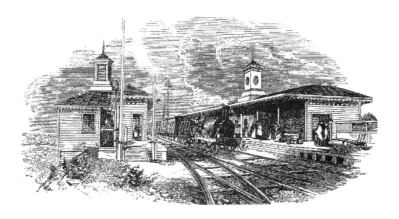

Harry Brooke sat alone in his First Class compartment. He looked out at the dismal grey tenement buildings as the locomotive hauled the train out of the station, eventually through the newer suburbs, to the west of the capital. So, Mr Brunel wanted his services for something else did he? Brooke mulled this idea over, what could it possibly be? What errand?

Brooke listened to the cacophony of sound during those early miles; the billowing steam and smoke, the mechanically rhythmic sound of the iron wheels upon Brunel's broad-gauge track. He could hear the sound of cinders pattering along the carriage roof and imagined red-hot coals in the firebox of the locomotive. Settling back and closing his eyes, he counted the minutes and tried to guess his location. He had developed this pastime as he loathed reading whilst in motion. The calculation of time against distance travelled was for more interesting: Westbourne Park - Old Oak Common - Ealing - Slough - Maidenhead, and there was Brunel's famously arched railway bridge, crossing over the River Thames.

He opened his eyes, ah yes, Maidenhead, the grey had transformed into lush green. He whipped out his pocket watch and checked the time, the train was punctual. Outside, pastures sped by at sixty miles per hour, then hills and meadows - grazing animals. The route passed through Twyford and Reading, a quiet town, nestled in the heart of Berkshire. He must have dozed, when he opened his eyes, having passed Didcot and Wantage town, the train was slowing to a halt at Swindon railway station.

There was a loud steam whistle and a series of violent jolts as the train jerked, thus announcing its arrival at Swindon where there was a statutory break, the duration of which would be called out once the majority of passengers had disembarked. Harry Brooke slid down the sash window of his compartment; leaning out to open the door, he looked along the crowded platform. Ahead he could see the driver and the stoker wearing bowler hats - grimy with soot, coal dust and the general detritus of steam engine combustion. The passengers, each of a certain social or professional class, alighted. It was a commotion of chatter and excitement. A barely-controlled scene of mayhem. A small boy had attempted to touch the side of the steam engine, he was immediately chastised by one of the dusty stokers; it had provided some mild amusement as the boy ran back to his parents, in fear of his life.

"Ten minutes! Swindon! Refreshments!" the loud, well-rehearsed voice of the railway guard called out. Brooke climbed down to the platform, clutching the precious briefcase. For a moment he studied the throng, searching for a face.

Rigby's Refreshment Rooms at the Station Hotel were richly decorated with marble columns, painted wall panels and moulded plasterwork figures. The queue for tea and cakes was frightful, the place was filled with families, noisy children and itinerant domestic staff. Brooke had wondered if there was time to both take coffee and use the Gentlemen's lavatory facilities. He thought not, and made his way outside again, prioritising the W.C., glancing over his shoulder as he did so. Vigilance was a habit from his years of service overseas.

He stood at the porcelain urinal; a man appeared to his right - the only position available, for there was a wall to Brooke's left. This sudden presence disturbed Brooke, maybe an odd lack of movement, but a presence there, all the same. The fellow was still and silent, he seemed to just stand there. Was he flexing his fingers? Brooke dared not look. He tensed himself, ready; every nerve sensing that something was not right; a natural survivor - responding to instinct.

Suddenly, the man jerked his right fist in a left arc of nearly one hundred and eighty degrees towards Brooke's face. But Brooke was ready for it, and for the brass knuckleduster which was clenched tightly into the fist. Brooke flashed up the briefcase to cover his face; an instant reaction, the knuckleduster connected with a thud against the leather. The assailant let out a guttural cry, as if the effort had winded him.

The pipe-smoking man from Eastbourne Terrace stormed into the toilet, grabbing the stranger from behind in a powerfully strong grip and roaring, "I've got him Harry! Disarm the thug!"

Brooke dropped the case and with it a chastisement: "About time!" He grabbed his assailant by the wrist, twisting it violently and fast in an opposite lock, the man winced in pain and dropped the knuckleduster onto the stone floor. Brooke's accomplice still

23

gripped the man who was struggling to no avail. Brooke struck the man on the chin with a lightning left hook; the man slumped forward.

"By God, Harry, that's done it!"

Others began crowding into the toilet. Out on the platform a whistle blew, a voice was calling out something about departure … minutes … hurry now …

"Let's get him onto the train," snapped Brooke, clearly irritated at this turn of events.

"But he's unconscious, Harry, and a dead weight at that."

"Well, we can't leave him here, and we can't miss that train either. Come on! Let's get a move on! Quickly now!"

Brooke bent down, retrieving the precious briefcase together with the knuckleduster. Between them, they wrestled the man out of the building, half dragging him towards the platform and the waiting Bristol train; a bizarre trio of men, one suspended between the other two.

The guard approached them; suspicious, curious, maybe a little sympathetic.

"Poor fellow slipped in the Gentlemen's conveniences," said Brooke with firm authority.

"Rather inconvenient, you might say," chimed his accomplice in jovial tone.

"Friend of yours?" enquired the guard.

"No, not a bit of it," said Brooke, "never met him before, but it seems he's in need of some assistance."

The guard nodded in agreement.

They reached the compartment door, Brooke, his accomplice and the guard all struggled to get the unconscious assailant boarded.

"Is he going to be all right?"

"I should hope so," said Brooke, "but could you delay the train for two minutes? In my attempt to help this fellow, I neglected my own needs. He needs some further attention, some water; we certainly don't want him dying on us, do we?" Brooke added the sudden severity for dramatic effect. It was enough to convince the assisting guard.

Without waiting for a reply, Brooke turned and ran back towards the refreshment area.

"Just, please, wait!" shouted Brooke at the top of his voice.

The guard consulted his pocket watch, shaking his head now for dramatic effect, as if the world might end if the train didn't leave Swindon precisely on time.

Brooke was back at the carriage in next to no time.

"I can't hold her no longer, guv'nor!" said the guard, almost frantic.

"You won't have to," said Brooke, flushed and a little breathless. He clutched a flask of water.

Brooke's accomplice and the assailant were now, at least, in the compartment, the latter lying across three seats, his right wrist handcuffed to a conveniently-located iron bar.

"Come on, Harry!" roared his friend, "This particular courier has a consignment to deliver!"

The carriage door slammed shut, the guard dipped his flag and blew his whistle, and the train slithered its way out of Swindon railway station.

Harry Brooke took a mouthful of the water and whipped out his pocket watch, dabbing beads of sweat from his brow with his silk handkerchief.

"Not too shabby," he said almost jauntily, "all of that, in less than four minutes. How's our friend there? He hasn't said much."

Brooke's accomplice turned the dishevelled prisoner, meeting a very pale face which had at some point frothed at the mouth. The eyes stared, open, his lips were thin and blueing, the pallor of cyanide perhaps? He tried both a neck and radial pulse. "Dead, is how this man is, Harry. As dead as dead can be."

Brooke conducted a cursory search through the dead man's pockets, finding absolutely nothing to suggest his identity. "He said nothing, and with nothing to identify him either, now that really is inconvenient."

Both men slumped into their seats, resigned to their predicament.

Brooke sighed: "Well you're the thinking man, aren't you, Peter - what on earth should we do?"

There was just a hint of sarcasm in his tone, his friend looked most perplexed. "I'm ... I'm not sure, Harry."

Brooke rose from his seat, now a little angry at their predicament. "We'll have to sort this out as soon as we arrive in Bristol. Get him to a hospital. Maybe that guard can assist again. I'm going to meditate and think on this; that little encounter was not at all what I'd anticipated on this journey. Of course, in the Army we could safely anticipate the risk we might encounter."

"Indeed!" Peter took out a starched white handkerchief, wiping the nose and mouth of the dead man, relieving it of blood and frothy saliva. It was a gruesome task. "This might be of use to a coroner in establishing the cause of death."

"Good idea unless, of course, it has dried by the time we reach Bristol," said Brooke.

"Yes, but under a microscope …" he let his words trail off for consideration and completed the task. He poured water over his hands from the pitcher, drying them against his trousers: "That's better."

Brooke settled himself into a seat beside his accomplice and the corpse. Peter Bishop could hear Brooke making himself comfortable, and within minutes he was dozing contentedly. Bishop took out a sketchpad and some pencils from his travelling valise, placing them on his lap. He focused on the face of the dead man,

"Now then, my friend," he said softly to himself, "let's capture your image before it is too late."

The rattle of the rails continued their rhythmic beat as Bishop began to sketch.

4 THE ROYAL WESTERN HOTEL

Bristol

"This is not the best news, Harry, not the best news at all. I hope you don't mind if I call you Harry?"

"No, of course not, sir," replied Brooke, although there had been no indication or instruction as to how he should address his employer.

"No, not good at all," mused Brunel, "you've allowed our only lead to die - our sole opportunity of discovering who he is and what he might be doing."

"With respect, sir, I didn't allow him to die. He rather chose to commit this act himself. It was clearly suicide; most probably a vial of strychnine or arsenic. We'll find out soon enough." Brooke sounded piqued at Brunel's attitude.

"And what of the character and reputation of your mysterious accomplice … Mr …?"

"Bishop, sir. Captain Peter Bishop."

"Ah! Yes, but of course … and?"

"Exemplary, sir, regarded highly by all. We served together in Afghanistan during 1842. Bishop indirectly saved my life there; I will forever be in his debt."

"And he vouched for you, at your court martial, did he not, for striking a senior officer?"

"How on earth did you …?"

"Don't worry. Guppy and I know the entire story through Arbuthnott's enquiries about you."

"The officer was assaulting his wife in a drunken and brutal fit of rage, sir. I…"

"I said, don't worry, Harry. And I meant it. I disapprove of warfare and I disapprove of bullies. It's just a shame you were caught in your action. Your excellent reputation sullied, albeit temporarily."

"It's an even greater shame that my commanding officer's wife later denied the assault ever took place."

Brunel sighed: "I suspect he threatened her once again, don't you?"

"Captain Bishop said he'd witnessed the assault too."

"Which, of course, he hadn't?"

"No, sir, he hadn't."

"There, friendship and loyalty, Harry - possibly the greatest of bonds of mankind, apart from, perhaps, love. What do you think?"

"I wouldn't know, sir."

Brunel boomed out a deep laugh. "Good answer, Harry, good answer! Now then, what about this business of ours?"

The two men sat in the private dining room of the Royal Western Hotel. The hotel was situated at the junction of Lime Kiln Lane with College Place, in the central parish of St Augustine's, Bristol.

The journey from Bristol Terminus, through the Victoria Street thoroughfare and into the heart of the city, had been fast and furious. The Hansom cab driver had urged his horse at full speed in order for Brooke to arrive in time for his appointment with the great man. Punctuality was a prerequisite with Brunel, apparently giving him a crucial insight into a man's intellect and integrity. Meanwhile, Peter Bishop and Adams, the weary railway guard, had

28

taken the corpse to the Bristol Infirmary.

The dining room was adorned with panelled wood, highly crafted oak and a number of paintings; some portraits and landscapes, and the most wonderful maritime scenes by local artist, Joseph Walter. The gas lighting was set low, and a log fire crackled away in the hearth beneath a marble fireplace. Positioned before one of the large sash windows stood a draughtsman's board, covered with diagrams and technical drawings of what appeared to be naval architecture.

Brunel and Brooke sat facing each other on either side of a long, highly-polished mahogany dining table. The candles of the table candelabra flickered over the remnants of a supper which had been prepared and served by the housekeeper. A crystal decanter of Madeira had been placed between them.

Brooke nursed his glass, waiting, and finally Brunel broke the silence, as if his mind had suddenly settled upon a strategy. "We shall study Arbuthnott's papers tomorrow and read those patent documents, after we have reviewed the unique floating harbour here in Bristol and visited my drawing office at the dockyard. But, for now, only one matter consumes my thoughts. And, it is a serious one."

Brooke sipped his drink, savouring the intense flavour of the fine Madeira, "Arbuthnott did say there was something other than the delivery of the briefcase, but he didn't say what - as he didn't know."

But Brunel's mind was occupied elsewhere; he ignored Brooke's words, concentrating his thoughts to the core of his worry. "A traitor is in our midst, Harry. He is amongst us, and yet remains unseen. This person reports to a foreign power is my reckoning; a spy, an enemy of this realm. And most certainly, an enemy to the interests of the Great Western Railway, and to me in particular. The subject-matter of the duplicity is obvious, the ramifications are clear, but the identity of the culprit is not. I will explain in full tomorrow."

"And the man on the train, who tried to kill me at Swindon?"

"The fact that he attempted to kill you, or at least disable you, must at this point be considered to be irrelevant. What he wanted was the contents of that briefcase."

Brooke flinched at this really rather harsh reality; but of course, Brunel was right.

"The questions remain: how did he know you would be on that train? How did he recognise you? He clearly did not anticipate the presence of your accomplice, who, it appears to me, must have saved the day. And, thank the Good Lord that he did."

Brooke was surprised at Brunel's frankness and fortitude - he swallowed hard.

"So, the treachery must have originated within the Blackfriars practice?" speculated Brooke after a moment's hesitation.

"We don't know where it originated, that's the whole point," said Brunel, "and if it was Blackfriars, why not attack you in London? The man would have saved his train fare!" Despite that tinge of humour, Brunel was clearly annoyed at the turn of events.

Brunel suddenly stood up, scraping the floor fiercely with his chair as he did so. He went to the fireplace, grabbing at a steel poker in order to stoke the glowing embers, his eyes shining in the flickering orange firelight. He seemed lost in thought at the hearth, then said:

"In fact, why not just attack Arbuthnott in Richmond? His age and disposition hardly compare to yours. You, sir, are most obviously a man of the world, not a desk man; a man not to be trifled with. As you so ably demonstrated against both your commanding officer and those two villains upon the rooftops of London; is that not so, Harry?"

Brooke decided not to respond to these observations and questions; he merely watched Brunel tightening his grasp on the poker and beating at the flames. After a moment Brunel continued, as if his minor fury and annoyance had not been roused at all.

"How was your journey, by the way? They're absolute flyers, aren't they, Gooch's Iron Duke locomotives? Two hours and forty-five minutes, with a ten-minute break at Swindon. But, we can do better. We will do better. One day, trains will attain speeds of over one hundred miles per hour! Twice that, I'd wager!"

Brooke almost laughed at this proposition, but stopped himself, remembering just exactly to whom he was speaking: "Impossible, surely?"

Brunel looked up from the fire although he still stoked away at it furiously, a glint of more than mischief in his features.

"Nothing is impossible to me, Harry, and you will come to know this. Belief in what might be possible consumes my mind each day, as all of my associates and employees will tell you. Once a notion is established, it occupies my thoughts entirely. I become utterly obsessed, and I expect my staff to share in my obsession. I work hard, and I keep long hours, and that's what I expect of all who work for me. Is that understood between us, Harry?"

Brooke was somewhat taken aback by these words: "I don't know, am I working for you?"

Brunel had more than a twinkle in his eye now, "Did Cornelius not explain?"

Brooke was being tested now - he realised that. "Only in as much as ..."

"I know, I know," retorted Brunel, cutting him off.

Suddenly the moment was shattered with a stunningly loud crash, like the clashing of sabres, as Brunel appeared to beat the hearth into submission with the steel poker. The sound was violent and would have been heard throughout the entire building.

"Got you!" exclaimed Brunel ecstatically, at the top of his voice.

Brooke shot out of his chair, knocking it over as he did so, rushing to the fireplace.

Brunel turned towards Brooke: "One of the embers was about to fall. You see, I can tell by the glow, the intensity of heat, its colour. Just something one becomes familiar with through experience." Brunel straightened himself up, still brandishing the poker like a sword. In the dancing firelight he looked quite a menacing character, his face flushed and eyes watering from the fire's smoke. Then, once again, his mood changed.

"Yes, Harry, from the moment you boarded that train at Paddington, you were working for me!"

Before Brooke could react or reply, there was a rap on the door, it opened before Brunel could answer. And there, standing before him, quite simply, was the most stunningly beautiful girl. It was an unforgettable moment; she seemed to glide into the room. Brooke was transfixed.

Brunel seemed not to notice her, until she spoke.

"Oncle! There was the most terrible sound, like the thunder!"

She cast a glance at Brooke.

"What? Oh yes!" said Brunel, "I was merely re-arranging the fire, that's all."

"With some vigour!" said Brooke, keen to be involved in the conversation and even more keen to be introduced.

"Oh yes, with vigour. I like this."

She had an alluring French accent. She looked at Brooke, then at Brunel, as if asking for an explanation of who the stranger might be and why he was there.

"Ah, Isabelle, I'm sorry, this is Mr Harry Brooke, here from London. Harry, this is Miss Isabelle Loiseau, here from Paris."

Brooke moved towards her, he took her outstretched hand and kissed it. He detected a hint of a curtsy in return; in truth, it was more of a dainty inclination towards him.

"Enchanted to make your acquaintance, Miss Loiseau," adding almost breathlessly, "and, at your service."

He retained her hand slightly longer than was necessary, their eyes made level contact.

Brunel, for all of his engineering skills and knowledge of physics, seemed not to recognise the chemistry that may have been occurring, stating: "Isabelle is studying music at the music school here in Bristol; she is currently on leave from the Conservatoire de Paris."

Brunel delivered the last three words in perfect French, for he was naturally bi-lingual.

Isabelle's eyes twinkled at her uncle, an intimate exchange which Brooke registered, but from which he was excluded.

"And what are you studying?" asked Brooke, fully attentive.

"Pianoforte, and I sing, a little."

Her accent, he found engaging, if not compelling.

"I would like to hear you play."

Brunel suddenly understood the situation playing out before him.

"Yes, yes - not now dear girl, Harry and I have matters to discuss."

She threw an enigmatic smile with the curl of her lips, "Urgent matters, Mon Oncle?"

Brunel laughed as Brooke released her hand.

"Oui."

"Well, if you are quite sure everything is all right, Oncle, I will retire to bed."

She gave Brooke one final coquettish smile in mild flirtation, and swept out of the room.

The two men eyed each other, until Brooke broke the silence.

"Uncle?" he enquired with a grin.

"Well, almost. Isabelle is my French cousin's daughter, from

Normandy. She is related from my father's side of the family."

"Oh, I see."

Brooke reflected upon the experience.

Another loud knock interrupted their discourse, this time it was at the main entrance of the hotel. Brooke consulted his pocket watch; Brunel glanced at him as four rapid taps fell upon the lounge door, a familiar tattoo broke the silence.

"Come!" shouted Brunel, returning to his previous vigour.

Mrs. McCready entered. Her demeanour had something of both the formal and the respectful, but her eyes twinkled with a suggestion of something Brooke could not quite place.

"A certain Captain Peter Bishop wishes to attend you, sir, at this hour, indeed!"

"Yes, yes. Send him in woman! This is important!"

She left, after admitting the new guest.

"Forgive me for intruding, sir." Bishop looked at Brunel and then at Brooke, who nodded at him in a kind of understated acknowledgement.

"Come in!" said Isambard Kingdom Brunel in a tone of voice that was clearly well practiced in delivering those words distinctly. For a moment there was silence, Bishop was clearly in awe of the great man.

"This is my friend and colleague, Peter Bishop," announced Brooke.

"That much I have already gathered from the effervescent Mrs. McCready, Harry."

Brunel held out his hand, which Bishop shook enthusiastically.

"What news from the Infirmary?" continued Brunel, in all haste.

"It was almost certainly a self-administered poison. The physician who attended ..."

"We know he didn't die from old age, Captain Bishop!" interjected Brunel, "what we need is some plain answers!"

Bishop shot Brooke a look, as if pleading for his support. He nodded.

"Yes, but strychnine is confirmed as the cause of death from the samples taken and the examination of body tissue: asphyxiation. So, it was heart failure, I imagine?"

"You imagine?" questioned Brunel, "and what does the good doctor imagine?"

Bishop could sense Brunel's impatience.

"Dr Percival Hartland needs to attend to this matter. He will be contacted as soon as humanly possible!"

"But, here's a thing, look," Bishop fumbled in his coat pocket, both Brunel and Brooke were attentive now, "these items were concealed in his left boot."

Bishop produced two items: a numbered railway ticket and a small brass telescope. Brunel took the former, whilst Brooke took the latter.

"Swindon to Bristol; that meant our man only intended to travel to Bristol, one way, from Swindon? So, he was never in London? I wasn't followed. That's reassuring at least," said Brooke.

"Of course," said Brunel, "that much is now clear. His ruse was to kill you, Harry, and then to impersonate you. I would never have known, at least, not for a while. The question now is, how did he know the significance of that Blackfriars briefcase? This was no random attack, it was well planned and intended."

At the window, Brooke pulled out the telescope, holding it to his eye, rotating and adjusting the focus. The other two watched him intently.

"The image is crystal clear; I can see the other side of the road in fine detail. Tomorrow, Peter, you must return to Swindon."

"To Swindon, but for what reason, may I ask?"

It was Brunel who answered the question: "Harry is right. If our corpse at the Infirmary had been keeping vigil at Swindon, he must have been observing from a suitable vantage point. Probably an upper bedroom at Rigby's Hotel, overlooking the platform, that would have been just such a place."

"But, it wasn't my face that he sought, no, it was that gold lettering upon the briefcase, the Blackfriars insignia," said Brooke, "small in size, certainly, but very distinctive."

"Exactly, too distinctive, and it is a lesson well learned. I shall inform Cornelius," said Brunel, "but the questions remain; why, and who?"

"Rigby's will have a record, a register," put in Bishop.

"Almost certainly false," said Brunel.

"But the contents of the bedroom may reveal something," insisted Brooke, "there is always something. A remnant, clothing, odds and ends, a minor detail that has been overlooked. And, there's this." Brooke removed the assailant's knuckleduster from his coat pocket and placed it on the table. Brunel seemed to study it for a moment and then dismissed it.

"Yes, it's certainly worth a try and there's nothing to lose in such an investigative exploration," continued Brunel, "as you have said, the proprietors may recall some detail we have not considered. And they might wonder about the whereabouts of their guest. So, that's agreed then. To Swindon in the morning, Captain Bishop!"

"I wonder if I might stay here, at the hotel, tonight."

Brunel smiled: "Go to reception, ring the bell. I'm sure Mrs. McCready will be able to arrange something for you - she might even provide you with a supper, with my compliments, of course."

Bishop left the dining room; Brunel and Brooke were still holding the evidence, their only clues to the mystery.

"So, Harry, tomorrow morning we shall take a cab around to the harbour and visit my drawing office. There is much I need to discuss with you; indeed, to confide."

"And then?"

Brunel turned to Brooke and smiled. "I am beginning to feel that you are a man I can trust, Harry. And I always follow my instincts. You might wish to pay a visit to the music school."

Brooke, despite his worldliness, could feel himself begin to blush, and this discomfiture seemed to amuse the straight-faced Brunel.

"I would indeed, sir, very much. Thank you," said Brooke, rather self-consciously.

"I am sure that Isabelle will be able to entertain you with some appropriate pieces of music. Perhaps, Beethoven, Moonlight Sonata, that's her favoured piece, and mine too. She plays it exquisitely - that's a promise. Please help yourself to the Madeira. And invite Peter Bishop to join you - he seems a decent fellow."

With that, Brunel left. Brooke poured two glasses as his friend reappeared.

"Mrs. McCready is presently warming the bed for me," Bishop proudly announced as he accepted the glass from Brooke.

"I say, welcome to Bristol, Captain Bishop!"

"I meant, with a bed-warmer, Harry."

"Whatever else? But, all jesting aside, thank you for all you did today and for intervening when you did. You make a habit of being in the appropriate place at the appropriate time!"

"Oh, I think you would have managed perfectly well without

me, your reaction was incredibly fast, almost as if you had seen it coming."

"Well, I sensed it rather than saw it. The fellow just stood there, waiting. There must have been some reason why. I mean, why not just attack immediately? It makes no sense."

"Let's hope we can establish more facts tomorrow," said Bishop innocently.

They chinked their glasses - to success.

"Yes, tomorrow," said Harry Brooke, but his thoughts clearly involved a grand piano, the dainty hands of a certain distracting young lady and a promise of the moonlight.

5 BLACKFRIARS SOLICITORS

Lincoln's Inn Fields, London

Lincoln's Inn Fields is the largest square in London and has existed since the 12th century. The current square was laid out by Indigo Jones during the 17th century and enclosed by an Act of Parliament in 1753. Nell Gwynn is said to have resided here and just behind it lays the Old Curiosity Shop, a legacy of Charles Dickens' 1840s novel. This leafy square is the address of Blackfriars solicitors, at the very heart of London's legal fraternity. Located in a Georgian mansion on the south side of the square, the offices enjoy unrivalled views.

A group of about a dozen staff members had gathered in the main office, standing with heads bowed, obediently silent and waiting. The atmosphere was positively funereal. Mr Cornelius Arbuthnott, he of the curmudgeonly demeanour and silver monocle, stood before this group with a member of the City of London Constabulary at his side. The spirit in the room was grim. A rumour had been circulating, but there had been no supporting facts.

Arbuthnott cleared his throat to bring them all to attention, and spoke without notes: "News has arrived by messenger that our trusted courier, Mr Harry Brooke, was attacked and killed by an unknown assassin at Swindon railway station, a few days ago. The Blackfriars briefcase, containing important documents created in these offices, is missing."

There was a collective gasp from around the room. Miss Victoria Appleby, a respected member of senior staff, a person beyond reproach with an infirmity which necessitated the use of a walking cane, was permitted to sit. She snivelled into a handkerchief at the revelation, her eyes red-rimmed as Arbuthnott continued his narrative. "As you are all aware, this firm has been granted a Royal Charter and has a royal warrant of appointment. We therefore represent not only Her Majesty's Government but, accordingly, the interests of the nation. Any act of malfeasance will be regarded as treason against Great Britain and her Dominions, and will be treated as such by the Courts of Law. The works of Mr Isambard Kingdom Brunel are of paramount importance to this country."

His tone lightened a little as he scanned the room, looking at the faces before him, watching for the tell-tale signs of any betrayal or guilt. His own years of military service, of meting out discipline and setting an example to enlisted ranks, had taught him a great deal about such matters.

"Now, there may be an explanation, I am sure no one in this office would behave in such a fashion, but the fact remains that one party has informed another party exactly when Mr Brooke would be travelling, and on what train. I want each one of you to assure me individually, during the course of the day, that no such undertaking has occurred from these offices.

Furthermore, no idle words should slip to a family member, a friend, or indeed to anybody else for that matter. It is essential that we find the source of this transgression today. It may already be too late. Mr Brunel's secret documents may already be in the hands of a foreign power as we speak. Port authorities have been notified and placed on watchful alert, but I fear the worst has already occurred. This is a very grave matter and I would be grateful for your co-operation. Thank you."

One by one, they filed out, as if in anticipation of facing a firing squad. Once their faces had all turned away from him, Arbuthnott allowed himself a smile. He was delighted by his performance. What was it Harry Brooke had said: why all the skulduggery? And now it was upon them, the dark forces were close at hand, he mused. He was the only person in London who knew that it was the assailant who lay upon a mortuary slab in Bristol, not the redoubtable Harry Brooke.

Arbuthnott folded the letter, which had been sealed and dispatched from the Royal Western Hotel in Bristol, and replaced it in his pocket. This tactic had been devised to have the following effect: if there was a spy at Blackfriars, they would report Brooke's death. However, the assailant would also appear to be missing, thus introducing some element of doubt. It was a triumvirate of duplicity and conspiracy which may have started at Blackfriars involving one of Brunel's trusted employees and a third party, as yet unknown. It was now up to Harry Brooke and Peter Bishop to discover that person. The clock was ticking.

A woman from the office approached Arbuthnott.

"Sir, the first member of staff, Mr Moffatt from Accounts, is ready whenever you are available to see him."

"Good. Send him in."

Arbuthnott rubbed his hands together; time to apply some subtle pressure and wheedle out the culprit.

.

6 RIGBY'S RAILWAY HOTEL

Swindon

"Of course, I remember 'im," said Mrs. Rigby, "'e paid a week in advance, no bovver. Didn't want no food, nuthin; we 'ardly saw 'im."

Peter Bishop held a note pad in his hand, although there was little of any significance to record. His Army papers had already convinced Mrs. Rigby of his authority, that everything was in order and that she should comply in answering his questions.

"Might I see the hotel register?"

Mrs. Rigby slid the weighty tome across the counter; Bishop scanned the list of names before him.

"Room number one, at the front, it's our best room, 'e wrote 'is name down as Matheson."

"Is there any doubt?" asked Bishop.

Mrs. Rigby shook her head in an unconvincing and non-committal way: "I dunno. They come and go 'ere, probably up to all sorts of business. But 'e only arrived three days ago."

"May I see the room?"

She nodded, he followed her up the steep staircase to the double bedroom which did indeed overlook the main line platform of Swindon railway station; all London to Bristol trains would have stopped below. The hotel itself was dingy and unglamorous, but potentially offered an ideal vantage point, he thought to himself.

Bishop opened the wardrobe to find a meagre collection of clothes, but one very smart overcoat. He looked at its lining, finding a label sewn inside bearing the name of the maker; Clarke's of Jermyn Street - a well-known and rather expensive tailor in London. It was curious that, whilst the other clothes were rather nondescript and plain, this coat would have been supplied exclusively. He searched through the pockets, finding a leather cylinder; a protective case for that telescope, no doubt. Flicking open the lid, Bishop spotted the mark of a German lens manufacturer: Leipzig.

"Do you mind if I take this? As evidence."

"Don't bovver me. Is 'e a deserter then?"

Bishop conducted another thorough search of the room without answering Mrs. Rigby's last question - looking in every place imaginable where anything might have been concealed, by design or otherwise.

"That bed there, that ain't been slept in," said Mrs. Rigby, "I can tell; maybe slept on - not slept in."

Bishop raised a quizzical eyebrow, but was clearly not surprised by this observation.

He nodded in gratitude for her honest recollections and made his way from the bedroom, heading back down the stairs to the reception area.

"There was one thing, though," said Mrs. Rigby, a step behind him, "I remember..."

"Oh?"

"'E walked with quite a limp, and 'e seemed posh."

"Posh?"

"Just 'is way, 'is manner I suppose, though 'e never said a word, but seemed like a gent. Lord knows why 'e'd ever want to stay at a place like this!"

"Thank you Mrs. Rigby, you've been most helpful. By the way, you may let the room again. Mr Matheson, or whatever his name might be, will not be returning.

41

7 BRUNEL'S DRAWING OFFICE

Great Western Dockyard, Bristol

Brunel and Harry Brooke alighted from a Hansom cab at the Great Western Dockyard. Brunel explained to Brooke the principle behind the creation of Jessop's floating harbour and the significance of its underfall and the system of locks stretching many miles further inland. He made Brooke aware of his own contributions to the harbour, especially concerning the issues of silting. The gasworks quay and the adjacent Lime Kiln Dockyard, located immediately opposite Brunel's drawing office, were quietly but steadily awakening in the soft early-morning sunshine. The wheels of industry on both banks of the harbour were slowly beginning to gain traction with the day. Brunel was an unmistakable figure in his stovepipe hat with his ubiquitous cigar smouldering away, regaling Brooke with detail after detail. Brooke was totally absorbed by this private tutorial.

Brooke took in the expansive view across the harbour, his eye following the contours right up to the terraces of Cliftonwood, perched high above them. Turning around, he could see a high range of hills to the south. He had calculated it to be of some significant height, as it was obviously many miles distant from where he was standing. His thoughts were interrupted.

"Now then, Harry, the purpose of today's meeting and your visit here," said Brunel, with a certain air of caution.

Brooke looked him in the eye: "Yes, I've been thinking about that too. Clearly, it's not just the patent documents I delivered to you from Arbuthnott."

Brunel could not resist a chuckle.

In spite of Brunel's private amusement, Brooke could see that there was something serious, about which he would soon learn.

"A red herring I'm afraid, Harry. And this is the real purpose of today's meeting, because it is a question of my immediate future intentions that concerns me most. Yes, a transatlantic telegraph cable is extremely important, but it is a long way off. I have already devised a method of laying a viable electric telegraph cable. I am also suitably impressed by a form of necessary insulation, newly discovered, using a gum called gutta percha - this will protect the cable from salt water erosion and marine life."

"I see, so what can I do? How can I help you?"

"For some time now we've had a plan for the construction of a massive floating pier, standing in deep water at a place called Portbury just beyond the river's mouth - not in Bristol itself."

"Its significance being?"

"Huge. Such a deep-water terminal would facilitate and secure the future and prosperity of the transatlantic steamship business from Bristol. The scheme would include a spur railway from the Great Western's Bristol to Exeter main line at Bedminster, a little way out from Bristol Terminus where you arrived the other night."

"With a corpse in tow. Yes, I remember only too well."

"The route of this railway would follow the New Cut, over there, to a point at the Rownham Ferry where it would follow the River Avon through the gorge. We've had these plans for a number of years now and had even formed a separate company, the

Portbury Pier and Railway Company, for this very purpose. We could provide continuity of travel all the way from London, via Bristol, directly into New York harbour. This goes back to the very core of my vision, Harry - a seamless journey - on ONE SINGLE TICKET; just imagine it, if you will!"

"And without it?" asked Brooke.

"Disaster, an unmitigated disaster for us, and for the prosperity of this city. Its shipping businesses will go into serious decline - for a generation, perhaps two. Without arresting the situation, it could prove terminal!"

"And you are saying that someone is trying to prevent this construction? The pier and, with it, your vision?"

"Certainly. My initial thoughts were of the burgeoning ship-owners and merchants of Liverpool, they have long coveted and competed for the transatlantic trade. For a company to monopolise the North Atlantic routes, that could be very lucrative business. Such a company would be able to pay handsome dividends to its investors."

Brooke sighed. "So, if not the Liverpool ship-owners, then who?"

Brunel lit another cigar: "A very good question, the answer to which I don't know. Since 1832, numerous plans regarding the navigation of the tidal river here at Bristol have been thwarted, for any number of reasons. Eventually, we were able to form the Portbury Pier and Railway Company and authorised to raise capital of two hundred thousand pounds, by the sale of joint stock shares at fifty pounds each, in order to carry out my proposal. We obtained an Act of Parliament in 1846. We were ready to enact our intention, the future of Bristol would be safe in our endeavours."

"And what has happened in these last few years, since that time?"

Brunel took a few seconds to answer, puffing at his cigar reflectively.

"In February of this year, both the scheme and the company were abandoned. The capital has gone, our personal stockholding and share certificates belonging to Guppy and me were stolen from the safe at my London residence in Duke Street, Westminster."

"Stolen? How exactly?"

"We cannot fathom it. Somebody has gained access, removed the share certificates, yet they disregarded ready cash and jewellery."

"So, the intruder knew what to look for and where it might be found?"

"Unfortunately so, Harry."

"Did the shares have a significant amount of value, may I ask?"

"Enough, yes."

"Sorry, that's not really my business, but I'd like to get a measure of the problem."

Brunel paused for a moment, considering whether or not he should divulge the extent of the problem. Finally he divulged, "Eighty thousand pounds in shares and bonds, plus other assured guarantees."

Brooke was startled" "My God! In my world, that's a fortune!"

"Yes, our consortium: me, Guppy, Mr Christopher Wainwright, whose fine Madeira you were drinking last night ..."

Brooke was still absorbing this information as Brunel continued, "...and Mr Nathaniel Bellinger, another of our shareholders, has disappeared although, worryingly, I have learned from sources that the body of a man has been found in London - Bloomsbury, to be precise - the description of which seems to resemble rather too closely Nathaniel's somewhat corpulent stature."

"And there are no clues at all about any of this business?"

"None, not a hint of a clue, Harry."

"I see."

"So, your task is to find out who is behind this: the whereabouts of the share certificates, hopefully, the capital, and perhaps even the fate of poor Nathaniel."

"There's a lot at stake here," said Brooke, his mind already racing through ideas and possible scenarios - many swiftly discounted.

"That's why Arbuthnott and I chose you, Harry, because you are undoubtedly the best in your field..."

He paused for a moment and then continued. "If you were able to discover that Lady Soames' diamonds were hidden inside her own mansion all along, then ..."

Brooke could not resist a smile at Brunel's tactics; a little flattery tickling at his vanity. "Forgive me for asking, but why doesn't the SS Great Britain, or whichever vessel, simply sail from the quay here, in this floating harbour, in Bristol? It's in the centre of the city and relatively close to the railway station, and it's only a short dash from your hotel. It's an ideal location, surely?"

Brunel stubbed out his cigar on the stove, this was clearly difficult.

"Oh, it's an ideal location, but the river is too narrow and too convoluted for such a large vessel. Bristol is also hampered by the huge tidal range, which led to the creation of the floating harbour originally. The Bristol Docks Company and the Bristol Corporation promised they would widen the river - they have not done it yet. It's as simple as that really, Harry; a catalogue of broken promises, politics and overly high dock charges. The route should be simple to be effective; London - Bristol - New York. We have demonstrated the efficiency of our steamers on numerous crossings to New York. My vision is certainly more logical than London to Liverpool and then down through the Irish Sea before heading out into the Atlantic."

"Yes, your route makes perfect sense."

"Guppy will be here soon. He'll explain the finer points of the docks problem; I thought you might be interested."

"I would indeed. I can now begin to understand why your Portbury Pier scheme is so important."

"It's vital, Harry, absolutely vital. Our rivals in Liverpool now have an advantage over us. A regular service and route can secure the Government's mail contract - worth a fortune to that operator."

"And yet, you don't believe the Liverpool ship-owners to be behind this?"

"No," said Brunel decisively.

"Neither do I," said Brooke with equal conviction.

"And why is that, Harry?"

Brooke lit one of his hand-rolled cigarettes and inhaled reflectively: "Motive; oh, and because the would-be assassin boarded the train at Swindon. Not London, or even Liverpool; unless it was part of a more sophisticated plan, which I somehow doubt, due to the sheer logistics that would be required."

"Elaborate," agreed Brunel.

"At the moment our only known enemy is the Swindon assailant - my attacker. And I'll wager he is the key to this mystery, dead or alive. And of course, we know he's already dead."

"Why so?"

"Because he wanted that Blackfriars briefcase, and he went to a lot of trouble to intercept it. But, he died for it. That's surely the ultimate price to pay, is it not? What kind of threat could hang over someone, enough to risk their own life for failing to obtain a briefcase? So much so that, as a precaution against this eventuality - failure or capture, he should carry poison. Something weighed heavy upon him, some perverse loyalty. Whatever it is, it has gone with him, to the grave."

"You make a convincing argument, Harry; you should have gone into the law."

"Into the law? No thank you, Mr Brunel, not I. That is certainly not a profession which appeals to me. Defending the rule of law, maybe, I suppose that is what I do really. But representing it, in the Courts? No. I find the practice to be a charade - theatrical, playing out a game when really, too much may be at stake."

"I take your point, I agree. The legal process is tedious."

"Indeed, but the investigation is not. Thank you for the coffee, by the way. I have rarely tasted coffee so fresh and strong."

There was a knock at the drawing office door. Brunel stood and straightened his attire.

"That'll be Guppy. It would please me if you would address me as Isambard, Harry, since confidences and secrets have been exchanged between us, which is a great leveller. And, as I said last night, I sense you are a man I can trust. Hence my invitation for you to attend my beloved Isabelle's recital rehearsal later today."

"Thank you, Isambard, that is very much appreciated. I look forward to hearing her play."

Thomas Guppy, the man of mild manners and quiet gentility, brought with him a large print of a photograph; the SS Great Britain.

"Isn't she beautiful?"

"Indeed, she is."

"The first photograph ever made of a steamship, and that it should be ours!" said Guppy with great pride, in his soft, west-country accent.

"William Fox Talbot from Lacock, a small place, out in Wiltshire; he is the pioneer of the photographic process. This photograph was taken just outside here, whilst she was being fitted out."

Brunel leaned the picture up against his drawing board with a similar amount of pride.

Guppy cleared his throat and pointed at the picture.

"She was our pride and joy," he said quietly, "four years to build and then a further eighteen months to get her out of Bristol."

"Really?" asked Brooke, "and why was that?"

Guppy looked at Brunel, as if seeking approval. "Well, as I mentioned, initially she was fitted out in Cumberland Basin - that was all quite normal enough, standard procedure. But, whilst the Bristol Docks Company had acknowledged the river needed to be widened to accommodate her and such similar ships, they had done nothing about it during the ensuing period. Then there were the problems of getting her out through the locking system; the width of the stonework - we eventually managed to float her out by way of a spring tide, on the 19th of July, 1843 - nearly nine years ago now. I can tell you, it wasn't an easy process. That's why she now sails from Liverpool, not Bristol. But she was built here, in Bristol, Mr Brooke, and she should sail from here - and, indeed she could do, if not for adversarial interference."

Guppy's emphasis and irritation were acutely apparent.

"Yes, Isambard explained all of the difficulties you have had with your Portbury Pier scheme and this recent theft of company share certificates."

Guppy seemed a little taken aback that an outsider was permitted to call the Chief by his first name, and Brunel seemed to read his mind.

"I invited Harry to address me as such, Guppy."

"I see," he said, his face creasing into a welcoming smile, "please address me as you wish, Mr Brooke. I've known Isambard for one hundred years and he still calls me 'Guppy' so, at your pleasure."

This time it was Brooke's turn to clear his throat with a nervous cough; two of the greatest living engineers in the world, were inviting him to address them by their first names! He was in very auspicious company, and at the heart of it.

"Before I take my leave to visit the mortuary at the Bristol Infirmary, gentlemen, can you just run through your list of staff, so I may familiarise myself with their names, please."

Brooke took out his notebook. Guppy rattled off the names and duties of those employees. Brooke scribbled furiously.

"And would you trust your staff?" asked Brooke.

"Every last one," said Guppy, "like sons and brothers."

"I would agree," concurred Brunel, "the entire Great Western Dockyard staff and those of the Great Western Railway are like a family. Trust is too small a word for a sentiment so great."

Brooke stood to leave: "Well, that is all most encouraging. Please be assured that Captain Bishop and I will make it our paramount business to discover the identity of your adversary and the whereabouts of your shares. Every effort will be made to reveal the truth of this sorry matter. Isambard, I will see you later, at the hotel, following Isabelle's piano recital. I can tell you, I relish that thought with far more enthusiasm than my visit to the Infirmary. A very good day to you both." With that, Brooke turned and left. Brunel and Guppy stared at the back of the closing door.

8 BUTTER WOULDN'T MELT

By the 1770s, it had become clear that the buildings of the Bristol Infirmary above Marlborough Street were woefully inadequate. The wards suffered poor ventilation. The structure had been incrementally enlarged, but without vision or a cohesive plan to deal with its increasing number of patients. There had been several fatal outbreaks of 'hospital fever', a mysterious endemic infection, probably due to a combination of poor hygiene and inadequate sanitary facilities.

In 1848, Dr Percival Hartland was recruited by Charity Universal as Chief Physician to the Bristol Infirmary. Hartland had been a medical student at the renowned St. Bartholomew's Hospital in London. In Bristol, he was fighting a losing battle in his cause to improve the hospital's facilities.

Harry Brooke and Peter Bishop approached the main entrance of the Infirmary and were directed towards the bowels of the establishment, for this was where the mortuary was located. It was supervised by one Oliver Maliphant, known to some as 'the imponderable parrot' for reasons Brooke and Bishop would never discover. As they neared the mortuary, they were aware of the sound of distant voices, of differing pitch and tone. The voices resonated against the hard stone walls and the subterranean foundations. And yet, Maliphant seemed to be quite alone in his cold, dark, dungeon home.

Maliphant, well short of five feet in height, was a dwarf-like figure, but was endowed with prodigious strength, and there could surely not be a better place for such a character to inhabit. In the gloom, his grotesque features were mainly hidden from public gaze. Dishevelled and odorous, he kept good company amongst his unfortunate guests.

This chill place conjured up images of wraith-like creatures emerging from dark corners.

Brooke and Bishop approached cautiously. Before them lay the body of the Swindon assailant, set upon a stone slab and, for the best part, naked. A cube of butter sat in the mouth of the corpse; the body was almost blue and looked stiff with rigour mortis.

"We knows e's dead, cuz butter wouldn't melt!" Maliphant said, hovering behind them slavering, mindlessly cackling like a hyena; quite plainly a person of low mental capacity. He walked away, his back hunched, he needed to attend to another of his charges - a huge tree of a man, but a tree that had been felled none the less, with ghastly injuries and spilt entrails.

This body lay upon a canvas sheet on the floor. Maliphant heaved the cadaver onto another mortician's slab as if it weighed no more than a baby. Brooke shuddered and touched Bishop on the arm as the Chief Physician joined them.

Dr Percival Hartland appeared to be exactly what he was: the epitome of an upper-class senior consultant physician. He was clearly fresh from his private consulting rooms at Number One, Royal Promenade, Victoria Square, in Clifton. He and his wife lived in an apartment above his practice. He was attired in a carefully-tailored morning suit, a stiff shirt collar and a silk bow tie fixed with a mother-of-pearl stud. He had a top hat and a decorative walking cane. Hartland was a distinguished gentleman of perhaps fifty years; his hair, silver-grey, swept back, with precise sideburns. A red carnation in the button hole of his left lapel did little to disguise the rancid odour, heavy in the air, redolent of death and decay. After all, it was a mortuary. He clicked his tongue before probing the body with a leather-gloved hand. He spoke without introduction, his tone almost anodyne:

"This is, or was, a man of some wealth attempting to give the appearance of a lower class, quite clearly a masquerade. A considered deception on his part, pure and simple."

"Dr Hartland, I am Harry Brooke, and this is my associate, Captain Peter Bishop."

"Who you are and what you may be are of no consequence to me," said Hartland rather pompously, "you are both here at the behest of Mr Isambard Kingdom Brunel, and that, gentlemen, is good enough for me."

Brooke and Bishop nodded in agreement.

"Good. Now, let's get started," Hartland snapped the fingers of his ungloved hand - an order to the troglodyte, Maliphant, who hobbled over clutching an oil lamp.

"The upper body, arms and torso look incredibly strong and muscular, disproportionate to the rest of his physique, But, look at the hands," said Hartland.

Maliphant lifted the corpse's right arm, to the audible crack of its rigor mortis. The sound was sickening, but Maliphant cackled with amusement.

"Steady on, Maliphant!" barked Hartland, "show some respect!"

Maliphant lowered his head with submissive humility, his deranged eyes darting from left to right, licking his swollen lips nervously.

"See these hands, closer," continued the good doctor, "soft skin, manicured nails, clean cuticles. I'll wager these hands have never performed a day's manual labour. No blemishes or scars, no cuts or bruises; the skin on the right hand is particularly smooth and soft. This man may have counted money, or managed some kind of commercial activity."

Brooke and Bishop inspected the hand of the corpse, as they'd been instructed, Hartland held it up with his gloved hand.

"The bruise on his chin is recent and accounted for. Now, show me your hands, Mr Brooke, I wish to demonstrate, if I may?"

Brooke held out his hands, obediently - large, with sturdy forearms.

"You are a former soldier, are you not? Artillery? Cavalry? And, by the look of your features, a well-travelled one too."

Brooke was amazed: "Yes, we have both served in India, on the north-west frontier, and in Afghanistan ten years ago."

"Lucky to escape such slaughter with your lives - very few survivors, or so it was reported in The Times."

"Yes, sir, it was hell," agreed Brooke, Bishop remained quiet.

Hartland made eye contact with the pair for the first time, as if a new level of respect had been achieved with Brooke's summation of the military incursion into Afghanistan.

"I've treated soldiers of the 40th Infantry and 2nd Somersetshire regiments. I've listened to their stories. A terrible waste of life, more so than any other conflict I can recall, in my opinion. Gentlemen, you have my sympathies."

Hartland carefully replaced the corpse's arm onto the slab and took a reluctant breath through his nose.

The arm looked mightily unsteady in its new resting place.

"The hair is styled most professionally, the beard has been shaven with soap and a decent razor by a gentlemen's barber - there are no cuts - indicating a well-honed blade, suggesting Burlington Arcade rather than some rural retreat. The teeth, although showing some signs of decay, are clean. And, there's this, found inside the folds of his shirt. The clasp must have come undone during your struggle at Swindon."

Hartland produced a silver pendant and chain from his jacket pocket. "It is silver, an unusual pendant bearing a French hallmark, dated 1798. The jeweller with whom I consulted less than an hour ago in Clifton assured me of its unique nature and therefore its value. You may take it. Show it to Mr Brunel, if you think it merits any consideration."

Brooke took the pendant and felt its weight in his hand; then he extracted an eyeglass from his waistcoat to examine it more closely in the dim glow of the oil lamp.

"Certainly, a very curious hallmark. The head of an eagle in profile, but what is this inscribed motto, is it perhaps French - Cur Non?"

"Yes. Mr Prosser, the jeweller, said the hallmark is of the 'Association des Orfevres'. Silversmiths. But, beyond that Cur Non meant nothing to him whatsoever."

"Interesting. What can it mean?" said Brooke.

"I confess my familiarity with France goes no further than the taste of a fine claret."

"Why would he possess such a thing?" Brooke mused aloud.

Peter Bishop spoke for the first time: "I'll take this, Harry, because I know what you are like for misplacing things - by the way, where is that knuckleduster?"

"In my pocket," said Brooke, somewhat piqued, "and there it will stay!"

Hartland observed the two men with mild amusement; he detected an air of unspoken competition between them, a friendly rivalry.

"Now, it's often said that you can tell a lot about a man by the company he keeps, but I would take issue with that. No, it's the quality of his footwear. How much money he spends .... Maliphant! Fetch the boots!"

Maliphant scurried off obediently, and reappeared moments later with a pair of knee-length leather boots of obvious quality. He handed them over to Hartland and waited for his next task.

"Wellington boots?" questioned Bishop, "that didn't register the other night."

"Precisely," agreed Hartland, "a good few guineas' worth. Hand crafted, made to order, stitched leather, and purchased so recently that they still retain the maker's label:

John Lobb, of London. They are very clearly different sizes. The heels are different too - the left has been raised by nearly one inch, compared to the right. Custom made for the client."

"How odd," said Brooke, taking the boots and comparing them for himself.

"Yes, indeed, Mr Brooke, how odd. Our man wears pauper's clothing to go about his clandestine business undetected, but he's unable to resist the luxury of comfortable boots," agreed Hartland, "and look here, traces of soil, or mud. This suggests a country lifestyle, or someone who has visited the countryside recently. No doubt an expert could identify the constituents of that soil."

"Yes, but it wouldn't prove where he actually resides," Bishop put in, quite unnecessarily.

Brooke raised his eyebrows, irritated at Bishop's comment.

"No, that is of course, quite true," agreed Hartland, "but, if you observe more closely, you will see that although these boots are clearly new, there is considerable wear to the outer edge of each heel. This might suggest some degree of physical infirmity, a problem with mobility or gait."

Hartland touched the left leg of the corpse.

"From my experience, I'd say this man was lame. However, the musculature of the upper body could be achieved through a combination of riding and rigid physical discipline; a regime designed to overcome his disability. Whatever it was, it did not involve the lifting of heavy weights - his legs would not have been able to bear the burden. My point being, he has been able to invest a great deal of time, as would have been required, to allow the degree of movement and fitness that was exhibited in his assault upon you."

Peter Bishop took the boots from Brooke, studying them closely.

"The overcoat I'd found at Rigby's was also from an exclusive supplier - Clarke's of Jermyn Street. The rest of his wardrobe was plain - very ordinary."

"And how exactly did you encounter this rogue?" asked Hartland.

"He attacked me with the knuckleduster in the public convenience at Swindon railway station."

"And in which hand did he hold the weapon?"

"His right."

Hartland looked again at the hands of the corpse: "Interesting, because I would say that this man was almost certainly left handed."

"In any event, although it was a cold day," reasoned Brooke, "he chose to leave his overcoat behind at the hotel. I suppose he was anticipating some form of confrontation, so he decided that wearing a heavy overcoat would restrict his arm movement. And he wasn't to know with which fist he would have to hit me. I was standing at the far end, next to the wall."

"Hence the reason why he hesitated at the urinal, Harry. Bad luck for him, he had to transfer the brass knuckles to his right hand," pondered Bishop.

"Yes, and that also explains why his strike against me was not as devastating as it might otherwise have been," Brooke said with a smile, "if you are correct about his left hand."

"I am correct," retorted Hartland, "if I were that sort of a person, I would place a hefty wager upon it. All of the physical and pathological evidence substantiates my opinion."

Dr Hartland removed a pocket watch from his waistcoat, prompting Brooke to do likewise.

"Well, gentlemen, I have other patients to attend to, but first I am meeting with Mr Gingell to look at his plans for the new Bristol General Hospital, over in Guinea Street. If either of you is heading back down to the harbour, you are most welcome to share the cab with me."

"I will," volunteered Bishop, "I believe Harry has other plans for this afternoon."

The three men turned away from the slab and the mortal remains of the Swindon assailant. The mortuary door closed behind them with a solid finality.

Maliphant emerged from the dark shadows, back hunched, with the hint of a drooling smile forming across his swollen lips and his eyes gleeful in the mirth he takes from his grim work.

"I believe Harry has other plans for this afternoon," he said, mimicking the voice and words of Captain Peter Bishop, with exact and uncanny precision. Then that laugh, the ridiculous hyena.

The imponderable parrot continued his repertoire to his silent, captive audience,

"Steady on, Maliphant - show some respect!"

Suddenly, behind him, the broken arm of the corpse dropped from the side of the slab, dramatically knocking over a bowl in its descent and causing Maliphant to involuntarily urinate - retribution exacted for the disrespect he'd shown to the corpse earlier.

9 A MYSTERY FACE

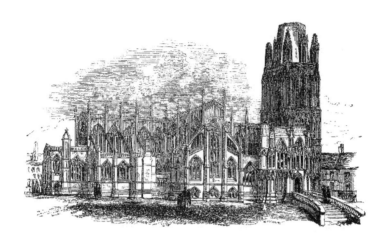

St. Mary Redcliffe is a substantial church with medieval origins which truly blossomed in the Elizabethan period. Queen Elizabeth herself commented on its magnificence during a visit - it was and still is one of the finest parish churches in Great Britain. It is an ecclesiastical monument of outstanding beauty.

"The finest," said Percival Hartland, as if reading Peter Bishop's mind, "and I, a Londoner, almost feel that in saying so I am being a traitor to Westminster."

The two men were riding through Redcliffe in the cab, heading for the Guinea Street destination. They both admired this famous Bristol landmark, Hartland began a detailed description for Bishop's benefit. He went into great architectural detail, encouraging Bishop to sketch some of the features:

"You should at least draw the inner porch and Berkeley Arch; really most impressive."

Bishop shot him a sideways glance of surprise. "Me?"

"Why certainly. Mr Brunel informs me you are, or have been, a war artist of some considerable talent and notoriety - for the Illustrated London News, amongst other prestigious publications?"

"Yes, but it's hardly the same thing," said Bishop, dismissing it with a hint of embarrassment.

"But you were on the move and very close to the action! What exactly did you sketch then? An example."

Bishop turned to Hartland; after a brief moment of considered hesitation, he made a calculated decision.

"You might like to see this, although, I've felt some guilt about it, ethically speaking - to keep quiet about it, because of its, its, ahem, rather unusual subject matter."

Hartland was immediately intrigued by Bishop's stuttering disclosure, smiled conspiratorially, "Show me."

Bishop reached into his pocket and withdrew a rolled up sheet of paper, unfurling it to reveal a pencil sketch of a face. He handed it across to Hartland who studied it carefully, silently.

When Hartland spoke, it was with well-considered words: "The death mask of a man deprives his face of some of its features in life - of hue, complexion, of a man's character, robbed of his identity. But this is, without any question of a doubt, your Swindon assailant, and his eyes were open at the time. I am sure you have captured a fine likeness."

"Yes, the man on the train," mused Bishop.

"Or to put it more correctly, the man you both put on the train. And that was where and when you drew this?"

"Yes, somewhere betwixt Swindon and Bath. Harry was napping, I ... I felt embarrassed, I suppose. I wiped the frothy sputum from his lips and dabbed away the blood. Maybe, I don't know, maybe, I shouldn't have done any of it."

"Better that you did, I am sure," said Hartland, relishing his involvement in this conspiracy.

"It didn't seem all that important to me, until our encounter at the mortuary, earlier. Then, I don't know ..."

"And that's why you were so keen to share this cab ride with me? To show me this?" said Hartland with a knowing smile, "and to discuss its possible implications?"

"Yes," admitted Bishop quietly.

"And does Brooke know about this? Or anybody else, for that matter?"

"No."

"I thought not," Hartland said knowingly.

Hartland placed his gloved hand upon Bishop's forearm, the hand which had touched the corpse.

"Don't worry, Captain Bishop. What you have here is a possible clue to an identity, nothing more. But our friend here will be inhumed shortly, for reasons of hospital hygiene as much as anything else. The mortuary was becoming somewhat over populated, as you may well have noticed earlier."

"But, what can I ... what can I do with this?" asked Bishop, feeling a little guilty that Brooke was not a party to these developments. But then again, he had chosen to go to the piano recital. That was his choice, his preference.

"I know what I would do, if I were you," replied Hartland confidently. "Consider this. What you have here is the living image of a man who certain people will recognise."

"In Swindon?" queried Bishop.

"No. I was thinking about London tradespeople. In particular, Clarke's of Jermyn Street, who supplied the exclusive overcoat."

"Yes, yes, of course."

"But more importantly, more specifically, Lobb's the boot makers. Those boots were of different sizes, left and right - as we observed. They were custom made. The man walked with an uneasy gait. The staff would remember him. Better, they would most likely have an address. And, with an address, you would normally have ..."

"A name!" Bishop interjected and smiled, shaking his head in recognition of that fact. All was now blindingly obvious to him and any former worries about Harry, the hospital board, the magistrate or the constabulary were now dissipating in his newly-found confidence.

The cab ground to a halt on Guinea Street, the horses struggling against the downhill gradient of the road and its slippery, wet cobbles. A light drizzle was drifting off of the harbour, which was only a short walk away. Above the surrounding buildings, the spiny masts of the ships clawed upwards into the dank mist.

Bishop withdrew the silver pendant and chain, holding it out.

"And I have this," Bishop commented, his mood had now altered completely.

Hartland climbed down from the covered carriage, buttoning

his coat against the inclement weather. He placed his hat squarely upon his head and, with a final readjustment of his clothing, surreptitiously checked his reflection in the glass screen, indicating that he still held a touch of vanity about his appearance. He smiled and said, with some emphasis, "That, Captain Bishop, I would keep quiet about, for the time being, if I were you."

They shook hands; Hartland looked down towards the river and up at the grim weather.

"I can't say that I shall miss this weather. Much as I shall miss this city and its fine inhabitants!"

"Miss this city?" Bishop repeated questioningly.

"My wife and I intend to travel to Australia later in the year. I have been offered the position of Senior Resident Medical Officer at the Melbourne Hospital. The gold rush and general migration have produced a greater demand on the medical services beyond their current capacity. But, thanks to a financial benefactor, what was once no more than a small medical unit will soon become a dedicated hospital capable of accepting one hundred admissions. There will be clinics, a dispensary, training facilities. Times are changing in the colony. It will be a fresh challenge."

Hartland smiled at Bishop.

"Is that how you know Mr Brunel and how the SS Great Britain is now about to embark upon the route, bound for Australia?"

"Partly it is, yes. We have enjoyed a very long association with Mr Brunel, Guppy and Arbuthnott, both professionally and socially. It is a bond of friendship which goes back many years to Isambard's father, Sir Marc, in London. Good day to you, sir."

In his perfunctory manner, Hartland turned and left Bishop alone in the cab.

The horses were snorting impatiently.

"Where to then, mister?" the cab driver called out.

"London. Take me to the railway station, to Bristol Terminus. Make haste! Oh, and I need to get a message to Mr Brunel at the Royal Western Hotel. Can you do that for me?"

"If you make it worth my while, I can do that for you, sir … Ha!"

A crack of the whip and the horses started to move off, jolting the cab around. The drizzle had turned to rain now, creating a very distinct and insistent pattering upon the carriage's roof. Bishop eased back and luxuriated in the moment. He would forget about

Harry's dalliance with Brunel's niece, Isabelle. For now, he had a capital role. And, it was his role to play. His moment. He closed his eyes and smiled in sublime satisfaction - all other considerations were now expunged from his mind.

10 ISABELLE

After the meeting with Hartland at the mortuary, Harry Brooke had walked from Marlborough Street up the very steep St. Michael's Hill into Cotham, where the music school had been temporarily located. With the deterioration in the weather, Brooke was grateful for the umbrella he had been offered by the delightful Mrs. Logan back at the dockyard drawing office - she who provided the office with a bountiful supply of tea, coffee, biscuits and local gossip. Brooke arrived in the late afternoon, damp and somewhat browbeaten following his encounter with Hartland and the highly disturbing Maliphant. He had wondered if Peter Bishop had been quite himself today as he had departed in the carriage with Hartland in the general direction of the harbour.

The main door was answered by a surly woman in her sixties, with steel-grey hair worn in a tight bun. Probably a widow, she was dressed in black, with an even darker expression. She led Brooke without further discourse into a hallway. The atmosphere here radiated a certain Regency style, rather than opulence, its space seemed accentuated by the omnipresent sound of the pianoforte, which echoed and resonated around and about. Brooke was led by the housekeeper into a reception room adjacent to the music room from which the sounds of the piano emitted.

He was greeted there by Mrs. McCready with a degree of propriety, presumably for his benefit, that demonstrated the level of conduct and behaviour deemed appropriate for such surroundings. The dismal woman left without further word.

Mrs. McCready was quick to acknowledge the shock of this encounter, which had registered on Brooke's features, with a smile. She now stood. She had been sitting, gazing into the open fire, lost in her own private thoughts.

"Mr Brunel had instructed me to await your arrival, sir, upon your pleasure." Her clipped Highland tones were evident once more in her announcement.

"And a very good afternoon to you too, Mrs. McCready," said Brooke, with all the charm he could muster. "My word! That fire looks very inviting, do you mind?"

He approached the warmth of the burning logs and coals, rubbing his hands together.

"And," he continued, "it warms one's soul, thank you. So, are you here to chaperone Miss Loiseau?"

She cut him off firmly, "Mademoiselle Loiseau is here to study music, Mr Brooke, not to suffer the attentions of gentlemen, shall we say. And, one particular, very worldly gentleman, I would imagine. She is vulnerable here in Bristol. Quite alone in a different culture, positively alien to what she has been accustomed to in …"

"In Paris, Mrs. McCready?" The comparison was as preposterous as it was untrue.

"In France, sir, her home. She has a responsibility placed upon her by her family to study."

"But, Mr Brunel is her family here, is he not? And in any case, he didn't disapprove of my coming here today; in fact, it was he who suggested it."

"I think you know very well what I mean, sir," she said, looking away, clearly embarrassed. And in that moment, it was clear Mr Brunel had given her no such instruction. Maybe Mrs. McCready was just being careful, if a trifle over protective.

The Allegro Ma Non Troppo with which they were being entertained suddenly ceased. But Beethoven's piano sonata Number 23 Appassionato now seemed to resonate with a soothing yet passionate intensity.

Isabelle entered the reception room currently occupied by Brooke and Mrs. McCready.

"Your uncle promised me the Moonlight," Brooke said in a jovial manner.

"And a promise, is a promise," she responded quickly.

"You play wonderfully, Mademoiselle Loiseau."

She held out her hand in greeting, which Brooke took and squeezed gently, his head very slightly bowed.

"But that was my tutor!"

Was she joking? Surely, she must be? But, he couldn't be certain.

"Come, Mr Brooke, leave your coat here to dry and follow me."

"I'll call you when it's time to take tea; you also have to meet the other visiting students, Miss," said Mrs. McCready, her mood now a little less serious.

"Thank you, Mrs. M, that would be most agreeable," Isabelle replied politely.

The Music Room was similarly appointed to everything else he'd seen so far, except that this room was dominated by the presence of a highly polished concert-sized piano, its lid tilted open. There was neither sight or sound of anyone but Isabelle being present in the room - no tutor. So, the piano sonata had been performed by her after all. Her playful smile conveyed and confirmed it all. He nodded in appreciation of her mischief. There was a double stool at the piano. Brooke was no pianist. Unless …

"Where would you care to sit?" she asked quietly, inviting him to make the decision.

"Perhaps here," he said, with caution, "then I may admire both the music and the musician."

There was a second piano stool. It was made from walnut, with a round, padded seat, cabriole legs and claw feet. It was designed to revolve, and was deceptively low. As Brooke sat, the brass knuckleduster was ejected sharply from his trouser pocket, falling to the floor. As it struck the marble tiles, its noisy report could be heard throughout the building and, he thought to himself, quite probably across the whole of Clifton also.

"My goodness!" exclaimed Isabelle, "Are you expecting to do battle?"

Mrs. McCready was in like a shot, her head wrapped around the door, her beady eye taking in every detail of the room, and of Brooke. But he had already pocketed the weapon and appeared innocent of any wrongdoing.

"It is perfectly all right," he said, thinking quickly, "this piano stool is faulty!"

Isabelle could barely stifle a snigger as she remained seated at the piano.

Mrs. McCready's head vanished from view, and the door closed abruptly.

Isabelle dressed well, this much Brooke had come to notice from their brief encounters. She exuded a certain style, which said as much about her character as it did about her wardrobe selection. Her hair was pinned up with a silver clip, and yet stray strands fell about her as she began to play the opening bars of the Moonlight Sonata. She started to speak softly as she played, glancing at him occasionally as if the melody might mask their conversation from the eager ears of Mrs. McCready, who was seated only yards away in the next room.

"My uncle likes you, Mr Harry Brooke. He says you are a man's man, but also a ladies' man. I am not sure, what does this mean exactly?"

Shimmering cascades of notes started to fill the room. Isabelle was concentrating, dividing her attention.

"I can't imagine!" was Brooke's guarded response.

"You are not married?"

"No."

"Neither am I."

More music; perhaps a minute, perhaps longer. Brooke was entranced by her playing of the piano, and by her. He found the combination quite intoxicating.

"And you've been looking at bodies, I learn from my uncle."

"Not bodies plural; a body, one body in particular."

She smiled as she played, the tempo of the piece had increased. What private thoughts at this moment, he wondered, were amusing her? She spoke English well with that beguiling accent. No other woman he had previously met had ever had this sort of effect upon him. She was very different. What was it about her?

65

"And what sort of a body, singular?"

"A very dead one, clearly," said Brooke without a trace of humour, "a man who would bring harm to your uncle and wished ill fortune upon his business enterprise."

"And you are here to protect him, yes, to guard him? You and your friend?"

"To help him, yes, in the best way we can."

"And why do they want to harm him? What has he done?"

"That's for me still to discover."

"Are you close to discovering?"

"Closer than we were, certainly."

Did she miss a note? Was she improvising? He couldn't tell, so intent was he upon watching the dexterity of her fingers and listening to her music. This piece of music was surely no longer than five minutes. He was unable to gauge the time, and neither could he fully concentrate on the music.

"That's not an answer," remarked Isabelle. She stopped playing, turned to Brooke, her eyes wide, seeking further detail.

"No, it's not. The enemy whom I seek operates from the shadows, unseen. I had thought it to be a foreign power. Now, I am not quite so certain of that."

"Isabelle!" a female voice called out, firm and with authority; it belonged to a woman who entered the room noisily. To Harry Brooke she paid no heed whatsoever.

"Mrs. McCready wishes you to join her in the dining room for tea and to meet the students visiting from Oxford," she looked at Brooke with disdain, "alone, if you please."

Isabelle looked embarrassed and mimed an apologetic 'sorry' as she stood from her piano stool.

"Your colleague has gone to London, Mr Brooke."

Brooke was shocked by this: "Really? Why?"

"I really don't know, but my uncle received a message at the hotel, from a cab driver. He and Arbut-something, Mr Guppy and Dr Hartland are all meeting to discuss such issues over late morning coffee tomorrow - at the hotel. There is news from the office in London. I believe somebody is missing, somebody important."

"Really? I don't like the sound of this. I wonder who? Anyway, it's not like Bishop to vanish like that without talking to me first …"

But Brooke was talking to himself at this moment; Isabelle had fled in retreat.

It was now dark and, after receiving some directions, Harry Brooke donned his overcoat and found himself walking along Elton Road, attempting to find Queen's Road. Brooke realised he was still some way distant from the Royal Western Hotel, located at the foot of Park Street, but at least it was now all downhill. Brooke decided that as he was not pressed for time he would find himself an inn or tavern; he'd calculated he was probably heading back towards the Old City rather than the hotel. There were things on his mind, he needed some time to reflect on the day's events. A tavern, a quart of fine ale, a comforting log fire, a cigarette - what better way to collect his thoughts?

At that moment something shattered the scene he'd just been picturing in his mind - he would never know what had persuaded him to turn around - was it the instinct that had saved him so many times before? But turn he did.

From the darkness there appeared two rough-looking fellows, set on some form of trouble or theft - one took a swing at Brooke. Their victim, his senses acutely alert, managed to dodge the intended blow. He fumbled for his pocket, feeling for the confiscated knuckleduster - he knew he had it there but just could not get to it because his coat was so tightly buttoned.

The second footpad grabbed his arm, attempting to twist it, the grip was firm and unyielding.

"Where's the necklace?"

Brooke was stunned by the question - this was plainly no random assault.

"What necklace?" he said, playing for time.

"You know damned well what necklace. Hand it over!"

The other ruffian came close, equal in stature to Brooke, his breath rank with rum and snuff.

"I don't have a necklace," cried Brooke, feigning fear, "search me if you wish! Take whatever you wish! Leave me be!"

Brooke unbuttoned his coat in theatrical protest, his hand immediately thrust into his trouser pocket for the reassuring curves of the weapon.

"Ah, but what's this?"

The man who had grabbed Brooke's arm relaxed his grip, but was still holding on at that point. The other fellow was close, but as he took a step back, it was enough of an opportunity for Brooke - at least a chance.

"Here!"

It was Brooke's turn to spring a surprise on his attackers. He turned, dropping to his knees and drove the knuckleduster into the first man's kneecap, shattering it. The villain screamed with the shock of such sudden and violent pain. The other villain, surprised and confused, relaxed his grip.

Brooke was up on his toes, dancing around this second fellow, the duster firmly in place on his right fist. Conflict had taught Brooke that the element of surprise is often the most effective weapon an army might have at its disposal.

"Who are you?" yelled Brooke, with fire in his eyes.

"Never mind about that - we want that necklace."

The injured fellow was writhing about on the paving slabs in great pain and distress. Brooke delivered a kick to the man's supporting arm, further disabling him.

"But what do you want with a necklace?" persisted Brooke, incandescent, red mist descending.

Anticipating another physical onslaught with the knuckleduster and in desperate need of an accomplice, the man still standing gave the game away, - shooting a nervous glance over Brooke's shoulder. A third man had been lurking in the shadows, waiting for this moment.

He drove a solid object into the back of Brooke's head. Brooke fell into oblivion in an instant, crashing onto the glistening cobbles.

When Brooke eventually regained consciousness, his head sore, the warm, pulsating trickle running down the side of his head, his ears ringing from the concussion, he knew he'd been in some skirmish. He instinctively felt for his pocket watch. Much to his surprise, it was still there, but he also realised that he'd been thoroughly searched - his clothing was adrift. The close proximity of horses and a carriage had helped to restore some degree of focus, he was aware of lamps glowing in the dark of the night, dreading the possibility that this could be bringing him further trouble. Brooke was dazed, confused, but acutely aware that he was in some kind of predicament.

"Mr Brooke! Mr Brooke!" It was the voice of Mrs. McCready and, seated behind her in the carriage, was a very shocked Isabelle.

Pillinger, the coachman, climbed down: "I saw what happened, sir. Three of 'em, roughnecks! But, they soon scurried off once they saw us a-coming down here."

Pillinger quickly picked up the brass knuckleduster, stuffing it into Brooke's pocket discreetly. So slick was he that neither of the two ladies noticed his action.

Brooke stood up unsteadily and stumbled against the side of the carriage, his hair was matted with blood.

"We must get him to a doctor at once!" Mrs. McCready announced and repeated, "At once!" as if to emphasise her concern.

"No, no, I'm all right - there's no need for that."

Isabelle composed herself, climbed down from the carriage, putting her arm around Brooke to support him. Pillinger offered a large handkerchief as a makeshift dressing.

"So, you were expecting to do battle," she asserted softly into his ear.

Her incisive humour was both dark and subtle and, whilst it was not lost on him, he was in no fit state to laugh at her remark. His pride in his ability to defend himself had suffered a severe knock. Isabelle took Pillinger's handkerchief, dabbed at the wound and applied some pressure to staunch the warm flow.

"No," she said, "to the hotel and make haste. A cold, wet towel with some pressure will reduce the swelling. And we must find him some brandy - for the shock! Come, Mr Brooke, lean on me!"

Brooke obeyed the instruction and together Isabelle, Mrs. M and Pillinger, shovelled him into the carriage. The word brandy had barely registered when he slipped into unconsciousness.

11 SILENT FOOTSTEPS

John Lobb was a well-renowned, highly reputable cordwainer whose London shop was situated in the shadow of the great gate tower of St. James's Palace. St. James's Street, traditionally the home of smoky coffee houses, gentlemen's clubs and fashionable outfitters, was a bustling thoroughfare filled with those going about their daily business.

Peter Bishop had dressed well, giving the impression of a certain social status; he showed the caricature sketch of the Swindon assailant to a couple of Lobb's apron-clad shop assistants.

"Why, of course we know him," said one, "that's Mr Charles Matheson."

A confirmation of the name, at least.

Bishop was surprised but clearly delighted at this early breakthrough. He couldn't conceal his glee at the thought of being able to present his success to Brooke, Brunel ... all of them.

He continued quickly with his plausible yarn, becoming over confident in his seemingly easy extraction of details. "You see, he left his boots at my stables down in the country in Wiltshire. I sought to return them to him today, since I am up in town on business. He'd failed to mention the address of his town residence, so it was very fortunate I'd spotted the Lobb's label, indicating where he'd obtained the boots."

This was an embellishment too far, and he realised it as soon as he had said it.

"He spoke to you?" It was the voice of Mr Lobb himself, who had just joined them at the counter.

Bishop was confused, but Lobb continued with a trace of a Cornish accent, his words slow and deliberate.

"But Mr Matheson has no voice; the poor fellow is mute."

"Ah yes, his manservant, you know, his factotum, had been speaking for him, of course, and had written it down for me," said Bishop thinking quickly, in an attempt to make the implausible somehow seem plausible once again, "but I have mislaid it since, and I wondered ..."

Mr Lobb consulted a thick, leather-bound ledger containing his customers' details, it worked like a directory and, thumbing slowly through the manila pages, each with abundant notations, he eventually reached the letter M.

"Ah, here we are. Matheson, Charles Edward. Twenty Russell Square. If you'd like to leave the boots here, sir, we can deliver them for you. Give them a polish and buff first, all part of our service."

"No! That's quite all right," said Bishop impatiently, having now gained the information he had wanted, "I will drop them in to him myself, it would be good to see him anyway, but thank you all the same. Good day! Thank you!"

Bishop turned and left the shop, almost with a spring in his step, supremely glad to have extricated himself from the hole he'd managed to dig.

Bishop walked to Piccadilly where he took lunch, in celebration of his good fortune and shrewd investigative skills: a Porterhouse steak, savoury Welsh rarebit and a half-bottle of claret - most agreeable, he thought to himself. He made his way on foot towards the Camden and Bloomsbury districts, feeling very pleased with himself. He tipped his hat good-naturedly to every mature lady he passed, and smiled warmly at every young lady. He was elated; he even gave small change to buskers and street entertainers - a custom he wasn't particularly noted for.

Bishop felt pleased that he had taken Dr Hartland's advice. Why, the entire mystery was practically his for the solving now; he'd show them all, back there in Bristol, a thing or two about sleuthing! He approached Russell Square through Woburn Place marvelling, as he always did, at the buildings and the sheer size of the square. Now he felt he was closing in on the villain's lair, or at least the villain's family residence. Twenty Russell Square. The address was now firmly etched in his brain, no mistake about it. He approached with diminishing footsteps and gathering excitement … 16, 18, 20 …

His heart sank like a stone.

For Twenty Russell Square was a hotel.

This was not the handsome private residence that he had been expecting.

Bishop climbed three steps and walked inside to be greeted by a haughty man fulfilling the role of receptionist and concierge, he repeated the same story he had used earlier at Lobb's.

The concierge took barely a moment to absorb the pencil-etched features on the rolled-up piece of paper. "Yes, I know the gentleman. An unusual gentleman. He has no voice. Walks with a limp. A cripple. Stays here about every six weeks or so. Gives his name as Matheson, Charles Matheson," he said, with some suspicion in his voice. The word 'gives' implied that he knew it was false, maybe he knew more, but would not reveal the depth of that knowledge.

"Yes, but do you know where he lives? Do you have an address for him?" Bishop persisted both gently and politely, although he was becoming irritated by the man's stiff manner.

"The gentleman has been coming here so long that he hasn't been required to sign the register since I commenced work here. He looked away.

"I see," Bishop was despondent.

"But I did happen to follow the gentleman to his place of work one morning, purely by accident sir, you understand."

"Oh really?" Bishop's heart was momentarily lifted, "and where was that?"

The man gave him an eloquent look. There was a small delay

while Brooke delved in his pocket and a coin or two changed hands.

"St. James's Street, near the better boot makers. But I couldn't tell you exactly where; he seemed to vanish. And I wasn't really paying much attention."

Bishop closed his eyes in exasperation and turned to walk away.

"Do you have a message for the gentleman, should he return?"

"No, no thank you. That won't be necessary."

Bishop walked out into Russell Square and sighed at this setback. A cab was discharging a fare at the hotel, the cabbie looked down at Bishop.

"Need a ride, guv'nor?"

"Yes, thank you. Paddington railway station please - I'm in no real hurry."

As he was climbing in, he noticed a newspaper vendor just along from the hotel. The newspaper carried a curious headline:

MERCHANT FOUND MURDERED IN BLOOMSBURY.

At the time this announcement meant nothing to Bishop, but later it would be a key event in the investigation he and Brooke were undertaking for Brunel and his consortium.

12 THE ROYAL WESTERN HOTEL

Bristol

The lounge in Brunel's private suite bore the atmosphere of a war council. Brunel had gathered together Thomas Guppy, Percival Hartland and Cornelius Arbuthnott for this meeting. Documents and drawings were spread over a low table and on the floor. Harry Brooke was upon a chaise-longue, his head bandaged, with Isabelle in close attendance occasionally applying a cold compress to his brow.

"It's only a graze," said Brunel, "do stop doting over him so. Mrs. McCready can look after him, should he need it. Don't you have to attend the music school?"

"Not today. Besides, Mr Brooke could have been killed," said Isabelle, positively oozing sympathy for the patient.

"Well, thank goodness I was not killed," said Harry, reaching for his coffee.

"I'll get that for you. Do you feel you could eat anything yet?"

"For pity's sake, Miss Loiseau," said Hartland, "he will live. And speaking of matters ethereal, the main purpose of my visit was to inform you that the body of your Swindon assailant, Mr Brooke, has today been inhumed in a pauper's grave, in Bedminster."

"I see, and probably a convenient outcome for all concerned here." Brooke considered.

"Surely, a man's burial, this is not your concern, Mr Brooke?" asked Isabelle.

He gave her a knowing smile, attempting to conceal this from the others gathered there. Brooke enjoyed the excessive attention he received from Isabelle, which the others could plainly see.

Brunel was privately amused by the turn of events and by his niece acting as Brooke's nursemaid. He smiled at the patient as if consenting to this developing relationship.

"So, they ambushed you then, Harry, the three of them?"

"No, as I explained, two at first, whom I managed to fend off, then the third came out of nowhere, from behind, with a brick the size of a house. My head is testament to this. And all they wanted was that damned mysterious necklace, which Peter has. But why?"

"Oh, poor man! Three!" said Isabelle, still fussing, "you are a chevalier, mon Dieu!"

Proceedings were interrupted by the sound of Mrs. McCready, knocking on the door. Her familiar tattoo, four taps.

"Come in Mrs. M!" Brunel bellowed in his usual manner.

"Captain Bishop is here sir, gentlemen, Nurse Loiseau."

They all looked up in a disturbed fashion as Bishop, flustered and weary from travel, entered the room.

Isabelle smiled alone, as none of the others had noticed the sarcastic address she'd been given, all too preoccupied with the matters in hand.

"The return of the prodigal son," said Brooke, now offering his own degree of sarcasm, "where the devil have you been?"

"London; and goodness me, what on earth has happened to you, Harry?"

Brooke attempted to shake his head, to dissuade Bishop from pursuing such further questions, at which Bishop frowned.

"I say, is there any chance of some coffee please Mrs. M?" Bishop flashed her one of his signature endearing smiles, all charm.

She returned his smile.

"Of course, Captain Bishop," she said, smoothing down her pinafore, "and perhaps some fresh bread?"

"Any luck?" Dr Hartland ventured an interjection with due caution, glancing around at the others.

"No! It was a wild goose chase! A fool's errand, I am loath to report. Except the name Charles Matheson was confirmed again; that's all"

Bishop took off his coat and retrieved the rolled-up paper from inside his jacket pocket. He flattened it out so that Harry could see it.

"My God!" said Harry, in shocked disbelief.

Thomas Guppy could easily have taken no notice, but he picked up the sketch and studied it carefully, his features growing more concerned. "And who exactly is this person?" he asked in his soft voice.

"That's our Swindon assailant," Brooke and Bishop answered in unison, although the former was clearly perplexed, not having previously known of the existence of this sketch.

"What of it?" asked Arbuthnott, "do you know him, Guppy?"

Guppy was clearly in a quandary: "Why, it's ... tell me, Captain Bishop, Peter, can you re-draw this image, only, somehow age the character - give it some greyish sideburns, some whiskers?"

Blank faced, Bishop replied, "Yes, of course. I'll get some paper and a pencil."

There was an insistent knock on the door; everybody knew it was Bishop's breakfast about to be delivered, but Brunel bellowed out: "Not now!"

Brooke smiled at Isabelle.

"But ...?" The muffled voice on the other side of the door questioned.

"Ten minutes, woman!"

With the exception of Brooke, they all crowded around the celebrated war artist as he made what was almost an exact copy, but aged as requested. He was shading it with the edge of the pencil. It was a fine job. He tilted it in Guppy's direction for his specific inspection.

"My God!" he exclaimed, "why, it's Thomas Appleby, one of the Steamship Company's most vehement detractors, and a spiteful, malicious competitor to boot! A man to distrust with great gusto! I believe he has a house at Box."

"Are you quite sure, Guppy?" asked Brunel. "Is it he?"

"Did you not say that you had seen Bellinger talking with some fierce rival at the American Consulate here in Bristol, a year or so ago?"

"Why yes, but I am, quite shocked, I mean ..."

Guppy covered over the mouth, only the eyes stared back at him from the page: inky-black pools - windows to the soul.

"It's quite staggering, the resemblance, it is the very likeness. It is him! I am certain now, yes - there is no doubt. It's the eyes. You have captured them perfectly. Oh, dear God!" said Guppy, he was both enthralled and shocked.

"You mean, this is the face of ... of the enemy? Of the dark forces?" said Brooke, slightly reluctantly, "you are quite sure?"

Brooke stood up from the chaise, took hold of the two images and studied them carefully. He continued:

"So, let me understand this correctly; you are saying that this man, our Swindon assailant, could be related in some way to Appleby? This man here, in the second image? He could be a brother or, more likely, a son given the apparent age difference?"

"That is precisely what he is saying," said Brunel, quite clearly shocked at these revelations, "you had better explain the significance of this, Guppy, to all assembled, for another thought has occurred to me, as I am sure it has to Cornelius also."

Guppy cleared his throat with a curious little dry cough and looked around the lounge, before he addressed them in his soft, west country accent: "The Great Western Steamship Company operated from 1838 until 1846, six years ago. The initial route was from Bristol to New York. As you are now aware, Mr Brooke, the rise and fall of tides, navigation of the river, all presented problems for getting a large vessel into Bristol docks easily, and there is no docking facility at Avonmouth. The dock company have not been helpful to us, they have neither developed the river-mouth site nor straightened and deepened the course of the river - just constant prevarication ..."

"Yes, and I find this to be a quite unbelievable situation," said Brooke, lighting one of his hand-rolled cigarettes.

"Precisely," agreed Guppy, "and all the while, the Bristol Dock Company would charge us twice the rate charged at Liverpool!"

"Meanwhile," Brunel interrupted, with vocal emphasis, "Mr

Cunard was awarded the first British government mail contract in 1839 - much to our chagrin! Not only that, it was even renewed."

The room fell silent, for this was obviously a very sore point.

"If I might continue Isambard ..." Guppy looked around at the expectant faces in the room. Brunel took out a cigar but did not light it.

"Of course, I'm sorry ..." his words drifted off.

"In 1846, the US Congress granted a group of New York businessmen a subsidy, an annual subsidy of four hundred thousand dollars, to start a steamship company to fiercely compete for the mail service between New York and England."

"To rival Cunard?" asked Brooke, maintaining a keen interest.

"TO RIVAL EVERYONE!" barked Brunel, "everyone."

"And it is the Appleby Line, which operates from New York, that receives that subsidy - it is an American consortium which is being financially assisted by the American government," said Guppy, "a government-subsidised mail contract to last ten years, based on a weekly service between New York and Liverpool, in direct competition with Cunard, which was already established in operating this route. There is nothing illegal about this, apart from, perhaps, an element of inside knowledge of the operating finances and such like. Mind you, they have increased the stakes, Appleby's vessels are faster and better appointed than the Cunarders ..." it was now Guppy who let his words drift off, allowing them to be absorbed.

"The fog is starting to lift now," said Brunel, "Thomas Appleby is behind all that has befallen us here - it's his family, it has to be. The Portbury Pier scheme would have given us the vital edge in such sharp competition, the route I'd envisaged: London - Bristol - New York. A straight line - the shortest route. Less distance, less time, less expense; we have proved it and had shown our colours!"

"So as I understand it, Isambard, your scheme, your vision was a threat to the newly-created American consortium? How could Thomas Appleby, or his American backers, have known your costs, your prices? Presumably, at the time you tendered for the mail contract, the Americans would have protected the US subsidy for themselves? But, all of this, in addition to the loss of the British Admiralty mail contract? "asked Brooke.

Brunel looked at Cornelius Arbuthnott who, in turn, lowered his head.

"This, for me, is deeply humiliating and most embarrassing," he said in almost a whisper, "because, a senior member of my staff at Blackfriars is also named Appleby: Miss Victoria Appleby."

"They must be related. This is no coincidence," asserted Brooke.

"Except our man was both mute and lame," mused Bishop aloud, looking around at the faces, "Is it possible?"

Arbuthnott took a very deep breath: "It is a lot more than possible gentlemen, for Miss Appleby too suffers from a similar physical infirmity. She must be his sister, or a cousin. This is no coincidence; this is disastrous. She is a traitor, and they are all involved in collusion against you, Mr Brunel."

The room went deathly silent as they absorbed what had been said.

"And I am afraid there is more," he continued, "Miss Appleby is now missing, she has not been seen at the offices in recent days, and is not at her residence in Portland Place. I have mentioned this already to Isambard, although I thought it of no consequence or relevance at the time. It has happened before, on occasions."

"Would she have access to papers related to your work with government departments, in addition to all these facts we have just learned?" asked Brooke.

"Yes, I am afraid she would," Arbuthnott could hardly speak, "but there has never been any question of her having any connection with America, or any Americans for that matter. As far as I know, she is from London."

Brooke ignored this comment, but pressed on: "And would these government papers ever be concerned with railway projects?"

"Yes," Arbuthnott replied.

"That's it then, Isambard. That's the connection you need. Somebody stole those share certificates for a specific reason, leaving everything else."

"They didn't need anything else," Brunel was mortified.

"It has to be Appleby, or one of his agents; perhaps somebody from their consortium," replied Brooke. "Yes, Miss Appleby is complicit, of that there is no doubt. And, our man at Swindon was a pawn in the game. Box is not far from Swindon, and that railway ticket proved his travel intentions."

"We need to find proof of this," said Bishop, "all of this is pure speculation."

Isabelle now joined in: "But how do you obtain such evidence?"

Brooke smiled and looked across the room at Bishop who seemed to read his mind, "Simple. Bishop and I will gain access to Appleby's house in order to obtain it."

Isabelle was taken aback: "Gain access? You mean to break in? Like, what is the word? A burglar?"

Brunel clapped his hands with enthusiasm and boomed, "That's exactly what he means, my dear! And this is exactly what I want to hear; words like proof and evidence are music to my ears!"

Brunel had become a barrel of excitement.

Bishop joined the mood: "Oh, yes! Right- ho!"

The Chief lit his cigar and stood to face the room, he addressed Brooke, but all of the room's occupants were his audience. "Did you know, Harry, that I surveyed every foot of the railway's route from London to Bristol - one hundred and seventeen miles? I planned every aspect of its construction … No one could complete the details, and so, I was obliged to do it myself. So level is the grade that the line - my line - is known as Brunel's billiard table."

Brooke smiled at the pride in Brunel's eye and of his anticipation, he was in his element; talk about pure theatre, he thought to himself, recalling his original meeting with Arbuthnott in Paddington, so very recently. "No, Isambard, I did not know this. But what thoughts do you have now?"

"My thoughts? I believe the best way and with most cunning," announced Brunel, "would be to approach Newton Meadows, Appleby's house at Box, from the rear, through the tunnel, in the early morning. Not by train. No. On horseback!"

"Why so?" asked Brooke, amazed at this suggestion.

"WHY? Ha! Because nobody would see your approach. If the house is guarded, which it may well be, the most likely points are the front driveway and possibly the sides. And, the day after tomorrow is the 9th of April - it is my birthday. At dawn, as the sun rises, the alignment of the Box railway tunnel is such that the sunlight shines right through it, from east to west! Timing will be of the essence, the small window of time lies in degrees and minutes."

"Fantastic," said Brooke, "is this really true?"

"Of course it is true, Harry. You will need your steely determination and courage certainly, but you will not require any torches or lanterns - the light at the eastern end of the tunnel will guide you through."

Brunel paused and scratched his sideburn, "I think it would be prudent if you both stayed away from the hotel until then. We have a friend at Cornwallis Crescent, you can stay there."

Brooke considered this, "Are you worried that the hotel is being watched? Precautions are wise. But the 9th of April it will be, at dawn!" They all nodded in agreement. "In the meantime, we might attend the horse races on Durdham Down. Pillinger mentioned it. Would you like to go, Miss Louiseau?"

Brunel sat at his desk: "I will instruct Pillinger to organise suitable horses for your mission. He is well acquainted with a certain local showman, O'Leary, who has a travelling circus. O'Leary has railway horse boxes in the yards at Bristol Terminus - he can load the horses there. We can attach the horse box as part of an early train, then rendezvous with you at Box, but you must already be there - this will be an unscheduled stop, there has to be the minimum of delay so as not to draw attention to any activity. You might be spending an uncomfortable night lying in wait."

"Good, that's settled then," said Brooke. He took Isabelle's arm, "Come, let's stroll across College Green, I'd like to visit the cathedral, then we can go down to the harbour."

"Oh, there was one more thing," said Brunel, "what happened to the pendant and necklace that those scoundrels were so anxious to relieve you of?"

"I have it here," said Bishop, "it was my intention to take it to Christie's, but I was somewhat disillusioned after the demoralising realisation at the Russell Square hotel."

Bishop removed the pendant and its chain from his waistcoat pocket and handed it to Brunel, who looked at it with interest. Isabelle stood beside her uncle.

"Aha, Cur Non," said Brunel and flipped it over for Isabelle to see.

"Yes, what is it?" asked Bishop, "is it French? A place, or a motto?"

"You do not know? It is a family, but significantly one person in particular," said Isabelle.

"But you would recognise the name, it is the motto and crest of a very famous French political figure," added Brunel, with an air of authority on the subject, "he fought with the Colonists in the American Revolutionary War during the last century - this is the crest of Lafayette."

"So, what is an unidentified assailant, both mute and lame, with a penchant for knuckledusters, doing with such an item?"

"Possibly it was stolen from a museum and he might wish to sell it; it is of no consequence, I am sure," said Brunel, somewhat dismissively, handing it across to Isabelle, "now I will begin to make preparations immediately. The 9th of April requires an early start. Good luck, gentlemen."

Brunel and Guppy strode out of the room with an air of determination and purpose, Hartland and Arbuthnott followed in their wake. The latter was still looking very shocked at the revelations of the meeting; humiliated by the fact that the treachery against Brunel had originated from his office at Blackfriars. And he, the redoubtable Cornelius Arbuthnott, had missed it. Despite his formal address to the gathered staff at Blackfriars, just a few days ago, at which Miss Appleby was present - he never anticipated such an outcome. It is now no wonder she had behaved strangely that day. Arbuthnott's frank delivery had unsettled her. If Brooke had been pronounced as dead, then where was the assailant who should have been reporting on his apparent success?

Miss Appleby had certainly fled London. But where had she gone?

Isabelle looked at the silver pendant closely and traced the contours of the eagle's head with her finger. "Lafayette," she murmured.

"Is it important?" asked Brooke, standing close to her, "what do you think? Is there a connection?"

"I don't know, Mr Brooke, but I think you should take it with you - it must mean something."

He clasped her hands in his, capturing the pendant within them.

"There could be ramifications to this, Miss Louiseau."

"Let us at least enjoy tomorrow, Mr Brooke, before you leave for Newton Meadows - are you ready for another battle?"

"I will have to be ready," replied Brooke, gently touching the dressing to his wound.

13 LIGHT AT THE END OF THE TUNNEL

Box is an attractive Wiltshire village right on the county border with Somerset; it is as famous for what lies beneath the ground as for the rolling Wiltshire countryside above.

Just beyond Box railway station, to the side of the main line, was a goods shed and a hoist. Before the west portal of the Box tunnel were a series of smallholdings, the mill, a loading wharf for the stoneyard, and a travelling hoist. And beyond the east portal, towards the hamlet of Rudloe, were some sidings that met a path leading towards Newton Meadows House - the intended target.

Brooke and Bishop had encamped in a draughty goods shed strewn with disused and rusting agricultural implements, close to the hamlet of Middlehill. They'd spent the night surreptitiously waiting in this refuge. The early train from Bristol to London would stop at Box and be detained for a short delay as the last wagon was uncoupled from the train and shunted into a quiet siding. Inside would be Pillinger, the coachman, with two horses at the ready.

Bishop checked his pocket watch. All was quiet outside as they killed time. "This is all too familiar, Harry, and it's not much of a plan either. We'll be relying on our wits."

"Yes, But, it's not like being the last men standing when there is little to no hope left, as we were in the tortuous retreat and withdrawal from Afghanistan."

Bishop sighed in resolute agreement. "How was Miss Louiseau at the races yesterday? You seem very keen, and she's obviously made an impression upon you."

"I am very keen on her."

"Is such a romance at all practicable?"

"In what way do you mean?"

"She is French. You are English. Her family lives, where - Normandy?"

"Yes, that's correct. Her mother lives there; not the father, though."

"And what will you do, Harry?"

"I don't know, I haven't thought that far ahead, but what about you, Peter? Surely this errand for the great man isn't going to separate our paths?"

"I should hope not, Harry."

"Did you hear that?"

Brooke peered through a crack in the shed. In the distance

there was a faint light, and the mechanical rhythm of iron wheels upon broad-gauge rails. Bishop espied the first light of dawn and listened carefully. "That'll be the train."

"Indeed, just a few more minutes now. The train will have to pass us, stop, and then run that last wagon back towards us. The driver will have his instructions."

"I gather," said Brooke, "that Pillinger has only briefed the driver, stokers and the Post Master. Several shillings will have changed hands to ensure a blind eye is turned. The fewer blind eyes required, the better."

Brooke risked a glance outside the shed door.

"The sun is rising! Brunel was right, there will be light at the east end of the tunnel. No illumination will be required, and the horses will be steady."

The approaching locomotive was now very close; its haul of eight wagons would soon be seven. A hiss of steam broke the silence of the early morning air.

"Good luck, Harry, old man!" said Bishop in his jaunty way.

"And to you too, Peter. My God, how many times have we said this? How many? The hand of fate and what it might hold for us? You have your pistol and ammunition, and I have the knuckleduster. What can possibly stop us?"

They shook hands, heading outside, their breath steaming in the cold light of dawn. Brooke and Bishop crept through the shadows, crouching along the length of the sidings as the iron behemoth pulled into the station with a hiss of steam, its firebox glowing with heat. Smoke and steam engulfed the unscheduled operation that was taking place. The train settled to a dead stop. But there were no passengers, there would be no witnesses. It was an altogether eerie spectacle. They jogged towards the last carriage and were not particularly surprised to see on the side of the freight carriage the words O'LEARY'S TRAVELLING CIRCUS. Accompanying the stylised coach paint lettering were joyous carnival images.

Pillinger emerged from the box carriage with another man, both were barely visible through the smoke, steam and semi-darkness.

"Pillinger! Over here!" Brooke commanded in a soft, low, theatrical whisper.

Pillinger introduced his sooty accomplice: "Frederick O'Leary, gentlemen."

The old man inclined his head respectfully, then Pillinger

curtailed the ceremonies,

"Right, we must get to it."

Pillinger and O'Leary hurried over to the train and began to uncouple the box carriage. Evidently it was a two-man operation, and speed was of the essence now.

"This is an unscheduled stop, sirs!" breathlessly telling them what they already knew.

"Who knows about this stop? It's supposed to be a secret."

The two men grappled and heaved at the resistant, awkward components; raising one piece, lowering the next, until it was unhitched. Thankfully, it was free and only just in time. O'Leary ran along to the locomotive. Pillinger wiped his face with a handkerchief of dubious cleanliness and considered the question of secrecy, "Just the driver and his firemen, the signalman at Bath ... oh, and the man at the turnpike at, that's not including the signalman here at Box."

"Not too many people then," said Brooke sarcastically.

"It would have not been possible without their involvement, sirs," Pillinger retorted, a little curtly, "now, will you please follow me."

They approached the rear of the slatted wooden box carriage and Pillinger opened the gatefold doors. Inside were wooden stalls with the unmistakable aroma of a stable. The two horses in it panted and whinnied, both clearly anxious to alight. Pillinger pulled down the wooden ramp and released the stall gates. He led each horse by its halter onto the grassy bank. Instinctively both horses began to chew at the grass, and neither appeared to have suffered any lasting anxiety from their recent railway journey.

The locomotive belched steam, the crew had re-boarded and slowly, very slowly, it edged its way out of the halt. O'Leary reappeared through swirls of soot and smoke like some unearthly apparition as the train began to disappear from view. Brooke and Bishop knew the sun would be rising somewhere behind the showman, and speed was required. The sun was now almost aligned with the tunnel. Pillinger was still feeding the horses clumps of grass, patting them affectionately.

Bishop began to make a fuss of one horse, "I'll take this one."

At once, O'Leary and Pillinger set about saddling and bridling both horses.

"There you are, ready to mount!" said Pillinger.

"They're good horses," said O'Leary, "they won't give you any trouble, fine mounts. The tunnel is three thousand, two hundred and twelve yards long so, at a good pace, it shouldn't take you long to pass through, ahem, beyond the sight of any prying eyes."

"Might I suggest, you ride in single file between the two rail tracks, that'll be better, it's mainly ballast, and there'll be no sleepers or ties. At the other end, before Rudloe, there is a sign for a church, up towards the direction of Chippenham."

Brooke and Bishop both nodded.

"Ignore that sign, find the one to Fogleigh Woods. Follow the bridle path and you'll see Newton Meadows House come into view. It's a grand old place, standing in its own grounds. Tether the horses at the finger post, we'll be up there in due course. There'll be nobody to disturb them at this hour. We'll wait 'til you've done your business, there's no hurry."

"Thank you, Pillinger," said Bishop politely, "but tell me, how do you have so much local knowledge?"

Pillinger looked back anxiously, realising that precious time was evaporating: "Sirs, I was born here. Well, Corsham actually, but that's near enough."

Brooke warmly thanked their two collaborators, and he and Bishop mounted. Gripped with a little heightened anticipation they looked towards the tunnel and, sure enough, there it was - a circle of light at the far end, shimmering in the early morning mist. Brooke checked his pocket watch one last time and laughed aloud.

"The finger post, sirs," said Pillinger, "we'll wait just as long as you need."

"Come on, Harry, LET'S GO!" cried Bishop, "I'll lead, but no cavalry charge through here!"

The two horses cantered gently into the west portal of the railway tunnel towards the light at the far end. Clouds of cinder dust and ash hovered in their wake. Pillinger smiled with satisfaction as the sound of the of echoes from the tunnel walls decayed away.

14 THE DAWN ASSAULT

Brooke's first impression of Newton Meadows House was of an excessively ornate structure in the baroque style, distinctly out of place in its surroundings, with considerable gardens and grounds.

The sun was now a red-orange colour as Brooke and Bishop made their descent from the bridle path to the boundaries of the Appleby estate.

"I hope there are no dogs," whispered Bishop. "they don't like me, nor I them."

He led the way down a grassy track, a cautious, silent two-hundred-yard descent which brought them to a wall. The area was roughly grassed and dotted with odd shrubs and bushes. Beyond it stood a derelict hothouse, its glass panes cracked and green with moss.

They were nearing what appeared to be the kitchen garden, adjacent to an orchard, and followed the wall of the kitchen garden, using the sun to give them a sense of their bearings. Now they could see some well-kept lawns. The early morning air was chilly, there had been a dewfall, and their boots squelched on the damp grass. As they approached the house, the surface beneath their feet changed to a gravel pathway. They continued to follow the wall towards the house - attempting to maintain silence. They slowed and approached the kitchen window.

Brooke flattened himself against the wall and very quickly glanced in through the sash window: there was an array of saucepans and kitchen utensils hanging from brass hooks, and he could see several large bread ovens. Bishop tried a door. It was locked, but it had a tiny rustic glass panel through which they could see distorted hanging shapes: meats, hams, poultry and game.

"This seems like a substantial household," whispered Bishop, "How many people do you think are in residence here?"

Brooke shook his head, pointing at another outbuilding which seemed devoid of life. It stood near a stable block, adjacent to the orchard: "Staff quarters over there, but who knows? At least there have been no dogs to give us away - not yet anyway, so no immediate danger."

Bishop grimaced at the very thought of dogs. He knelt, offering up a silent prayer, and started to probe the lock, trying to manipulate it with a skeleton key. It clicked decisively and the door opened inwards, with the squeak of unoiled hinges and weathered wood. Bishop eased it open still further, enough for them both to squeeze through.

Once inside they waited, listening for any sounds, absorbing the atmosphere of their surroundings for any tell-tale clues. This was an old habit, born of experience. Brooke closed his eyes, concentrating, considering each tiny detail, his imagination alive with possibilities. Danger could not be far away either.

"The servants are up; that smelled like wood smoke coming from the chimneys," he whispered, opening his eyes, "shall we?"

Brooke nodded, his nostrils flared once again as he took in every detail; a survivor - listening and responding to his instincts. "Is it too quiet?" he whispered.

They crept out of the kitchen and into a tiled hallway with mullion glass windows, oak-panelled walls and a high, very ornate plasterwork ceiling. The staircase led up to a gallery with arched openings. Doors to the upper rooms were visible. The gallery walls were adorned with paintings; works of art more appropriate to a museum than a private house.

They stopped again and listened. What was that sound that had suddenly made them so cautious? They heard the metronomic pendulum of a long-case clock somewhere within the house, the crackle of a wood fire but, definitely, there was something else. Could it be a dog? Bishop wondered. Some great canine creature, stretching and yawning on its bed, suddenly aware of an intrusion of fresh scent into its familiar world?

Yawning? No, that wasn't yawning - it was snoring.

They entered a grand reception room, a state room of severe grandeur and proportions in the midst of a collision of styles: Rococo plasterwork ceiling, ornate pillars of carved wood, and richly-upholstered furniture.

But the room had a theme. There was the American Union flag, and above the fireplace was the portrait of a man gazing out over the room with an all-seeing eye. It was George Washington, the first President of the United States of America and Commander in Chief of the Colonial Forces during the American Revolutionary War. Another painting, not quite so prominent, depicted Lord Cornwallis and the British surrender at Yorktown in 1781. Other painted scenes showed the settlements at Plymouth, Massachusetts of those early Pilgrim refugees, the Brethren.

The snoring stopped: there was an audible mechanical click, the unmistakable metallic sound of a weapon being cocked, and a voice. "Howdy. You're earlier than I expected, but how did you get in? I have men out there, waiting …"

The man paused, annoyed.

"But, no matter. I'm holding a Colt Walker Forty-Four revolver, and it is directed at your face. I have another beside me. That's twelve shots in all. Give me one good reason why I shouldn't just kill the both of you right now."

And there it was. The face of the Swindon assailant; strangely familiar, if a little older and a little more lined, but with the same eyes - cold, black, vindictive. This man had sharp facial features, thin lizard-like lips, a high forehead with a haughty expression. But the eyes - cold dark pools, ready to kill. Bishop's drawing had captured and frozen that sneer of superiority utterly.

Thomas Appleby was wearing a bulky scarlet-coloured tunic, fully buttoned, with military insignia at the rounded collar. He seemed to have appeared out of thin air, near a large ornate couch. His accent was curious and unfamiliar. It wasn't local, but, at the same time it sounded vaguely of the west country.

Bishop attempted to put his hand inside his coat pocket.

"No, no, no! You see with this Forty-Four I can take you both down; why, you are trespassing upon my property."

"I'm not armed," Bishop lied, too quickly, too stupidly.

"Oh, yes y'are."

Brooke listened intently and watched Appleby carefully.

He was a big man; muscular, fair-haired with a complexion that was no stranger to the sun.

"Is it holstered? And like any other self respectin' soldier, you've kept it clean, oiled and ready for use?"

"Yes," replied Bishop and in that one word, his tone admitted defeat.

"Well it ain't no use there. So, unbutton your coat, slowly, so as I can see, and put the gun down on this here desk. And don't you scratch it. It's American walnut."

Appleby advanced towards his intruders and the desk; he gripped the revolver, signalling his intent in no uncertain terms. This was Bishop's sketch and the Swindon assailant in a single form, but this being was neither lame nor mute.

Bishop carefully placed his weapon onto the desk without breaking eye contact with Appleby. Appleby nodded, as if in approval, something private that he did not care to share. His face folded into a smile; it was the assurance of a man who knows he has control, knowing he has outwitted his adversaries. And satisfyingly, with so much ease.

"Might be a thrill to kill y'all anyway, but I am curious … what do you want? The game is done. I won. Brunel lost. End." He locked Bishop's gun in the drawer of the desk, withdrawing the key, smiling broadly as he did so, "You want to kill me? That's not gonna happen."

Brooke spoke for the first time during this encounter, he realised the position in which they now found themselves was desperate, his voice rasped from the transition from the cold air outside into the smoky warmth of this room. "How about this?"

He held out his left hand, fist clenched, turned it over and opened his palm towards Appleby. The silver pendant glinted softly in the fire's light.

"Cur Non? Lafayette?" Brooke spat out his words in a tone that may have implied some provocation.

Appleby's face furrowed. Confusion, then a dawning shock. His pace accelerated, his eyes darting from the pendant to his foe, still tightly gripping his pistol. He wasn't going to be fooled. The situation was becoming ever more dangerous, but Appleby's disbelief was palpable. "The hell did you get that?" he shouted. "Put it on the desk!"

Brooke obeyed. "A man sold it to me, on the train - he said he wanted two guineas for it."

"He said? No, he said nothing to you." Appleby's voice was firm, his temper clearly rattled. His steadfast control was beginning to ebb. He turned to the desk, picking up the pendant carefully with his left hand. "The train," he continued, "the train? Oh, so you must be Brooke ... the dead courier ... ha!"

Appleby scratched his chin and laughed: "You evaded my men in Bristol. God damn nearly killed one of them. You didn't realise the Applebys are smart. We have eyes everywhere. Watchers, I call them."

"Really?" said Brooke, unimpressed, "I should hire some better ones, if I were you."

Appleby snapped and shouted: "Where is my son?"

For a moment Brooke and Bishop ignored him; then he shouted the question again on the brink of rage.

Casually, Brooke announced, "He's dead ... and, already buried."

Appleby's countenance glared: "Dead, how?"

Brooke and Bishop continued their silence until Appleby shouted once again: "HOW?"

It was Bishop who answered, again there was a casual air in his voice: "He took his own life; he poisoned himself."

"NO! NO!" an angst-ridden cry, Appleby's defences had been breached.

Bishop continued his dismissive nonchalance: "Yes. And, I must ask; if he was your son - by his actions, what sort of a father does that make you, exactly?"

Appleby was spellbound: "What did you say?"

Bishop's tone became uncharacteristically cruel. Brooke watched him carefully, fully aware of what Bishop was attempting to achieve.

"Faced with failure, your son chose death rather than letting his failure be known to you. That must be a bitter truth to swallow, even for you. So, why?"

Brooke knew Bishop was playing with fire and tried to interject: "Peter, I ..."

Bishop shouted him down: "Well, it's true. Suicide. The action taken by a coward, choosing death over living with the reality of his failure ..."

In that split second, Bishop aimed a violent kick towards Appleby's left kneecap with a fluid movement: decisive, unexpected and very quick. But not quick enough. Appleby immediately stepped back, cocked the hammer, aimed and fired with an equally fluid and rapid reaction, his eyes cold, dark and murderous. It all happened within two seconds. The gun's explosion was absolutely deafening. Its shattering report echoed around the walls. Brooke instantly covered his ears.

The Colt's bullet caught Bishop firmly in the crease of his left shoulder. At such close range, the sheer power of its impact spun him around, Bishop fell back clutching at his chest.

"No! Peter!" cried Brooke.

Bishop crashed to the floor, his arms sprawling limply. Brooke's thoughts raced; God, was it an artery or his lung? He wasn't a medical man, but he knew only too well that sudden shock, such intense trauma and loss of blood, was almost always fatal and there was not going to be any emergency first aid administered in these circumstances.

Brooke was confused; his ears were ringing with the gun's report. Could he help his friend or should he attempt to tackle Appleby? He chose the latter, but his indecision had cost him vital time and he was looking down the barrel of a smoking gun. Appleby's hand was steady. No remorse. No fear. Just a cold sneer. He was the victor in this gladiatorial struggle.

This could only end in death.

Brooke turned.

"Easy, Mr Brooke, no hasty moves or you'll get the same. Understand?"

"God damn you, Appleby."

"Probably he will, yes. But then, I have other advantages on my side, and they are certainly not spiritual."

Bishop, his friend, his companion; the man who had once saved

93

his life, was dying before him, crumpled and defeated. Brooke knew it was a useless situation, but he knelt beside him, taking his hand. A thousand memories flashed through his mind. Bishop was pale, his life seeping away with the flow of his blood - he knew he was dying.

"Peter … Peter," Brooke's words sounded hollow and strained, he could barely bring himself to speak.

"I'm sorry, old man," Bishop's familiar manner, "I've rather let you down this time," a glimmer of a smile seemed to settle on his face before his head slumped to the side, and silence.

"Never … you've never let me down," whispered Brooke, to his dead friend. He leaned back, assessing his options.

The air was acrid from cordite, bristling with tension and charged with emotion, but Appleby's Colt was still unerringly trained upon him.

"You'll pay for this Appleby," said Brooke, fighting back tears of rage.

"Not from where I'm standing," was Appleby's pompous reply, "always ensure I have the upper hand … now, stand up Mr Brooke … nice and slow … that's it and keep your hands where I can see them."

"What's going on here?" It was the voice of a woman, who had descended the stairs with obvious difficulty. There was the rhythmic beat of a walking cane: tap, tap, tap.

Miss Victoria Appleby.

"We had intruders. I was compelled to take care of one."

Brooke desperately tried to compose himself: "So, you are the poison that infiltrated Blackfriars - the traitor. I wondered what you might look like, but you'll be judged for the treachery of your actions, rather than on your appearance."

"Don't make it any more difficult, Brooke, I'm the one with the gun here. And you, you have nothing. Nothing."

"DIFFICULT?" shouted Brooke, spitting the words out, "you've just killed Bishop."

Appleby's words were becoming ever more spiteful, mimicking Bishop's dying words and tone: "Self defence - sorry, old man - you are the intruders, after all."

Brooke rose, facing them both. "Miss Appleby, yes Arbuthnott told us all about you. He's known for a long time now that you've been passing confidential information on to someone; it just took us a while to work out exactly who."

She laughed in his face: "NONSENSE! Arbuthnott is stupid, pompous and arrogant. A fool. Too full of his own self-importance; he knows nothing and neither do you."

Brooke waited for a moment, carefully timing his response; needing something that he knew neither of them could answer: "Then why do you think that we are here? And how do you think we knew exactly where to find you both? You gave yourselves away, long ago, you left a trail and we followed it here, all the way to Newton Meadows."

She turned to Thomas Appleby, dumbfounded: "I, I really don't ..."

Brooke pounced on her momentary weakness, he sensed there was an element of doubt neither of them had considered: "Of course you are a traitor. You stole Brunel's plans, copied his private documents. You broke into his house in Duke Street. I KNOW YOU DID. Brunel has told me."

"Not I. No. But Charles did - on his visits to London."

"Charles Matheson?" Brooke pondered, "I see, so he was actually Charles Appleby."

"He entered the Duke Street residence through its attic, from the property next door, to look at the plans and letters. Charles had a fantastic memory. He could read pages of letters from Gooch, from Emma Harrison, Paxton, Telford, even Guppy. He could reproduce detailed diagrams and plans without the need to steal them ... He would return here and recite their contents verbatim." Appleby stated it with a measure of pride.

Brooke was visibly confused: "Recite? I thought..."

"Just like me, Charles was born and raised in America, and he lived there until relatively recently. He too spoke with a strong American accent. It wouldn't do to have such a person roaming at large, attracting too much unwanted attention; tensions between the nations - too many uncomfortable questions. I can get away with it, I've lived here for many years and I can mimic the English country accent. The fools just think me eccentric."

The last words were spoken in a convincing dialect that may have originated in Wiltshire, Somerset or Gloucestershire.

"And his physical infirmity? Or was that faked too?"

"Infantile paralysis, what my sister here has to suffer. Not sure how it comes about."

"Well, since it is your intention to kill me anyway, you might just answer one question." Brooke moved away from Bishop's body, towards the fireplace and the unfurled flag of the American Union. He was manoeuvring himself into a better position and using the questions as a distraction.

"Go on," Appleby relaxed his grip on the revolver, just a fraction, but his dark eyes remained focussed and unforgiving.

"How did your thugs know where I was that night?"

Appleby laughed: "Why, they followed you, of course. My watchers were instructed to find you, kill you and get the Lafayette pendant. Simple. The eyes, I already told you." He took a breath and sneered with contempt. "They watch Brunel's hotel, his drawing office; and why, yes, The Music Academy too. My she's a pretty little thing ain't she. Bit out of your league though Brooke, huh?"

Brooke didn't rise to the bait: "You don't impress me. Not one bit."

Appleby tightened his grip on the weapon again: "You think I care?"

"All right," said Brooke, "change of tack. Why do you want that pendant?"

"Why?" he shouted, "Isn't it obvious? Because that pendant had belonged to Lafayette - for us, he is a hero. He defeated the British and gave Americans their rightful freedom - all of them. No taxation without representation. My father died for the cause, in the war of 1812, fighting the English."

Appleby went to the desk and picked up the pendant.

"It's not about the material value of this, but its symbolism, that's its true significance. I wondered why Charles had taken it with him, but it looks as if I have it back now, anyway."

Brooke watched him put it back on the table.

"What is all of this about then?" asked Brooke.

Appleby took a deep breath and for a moment looked around the room, time was his. Brooke watched Appleby carefully.

Appleby smirked: "Why, I don't believe I am disposed to tell you. I don't need to. I don't have to. I don't want to. You're a dead man, Brooke, just like your friend there."

Appleby started to walk away, apparently unmoved by his slaying of Bishop.

"Greed," Brooke suggested, "plain greed. This was not about

winning a struggle of arms, or a revolution. The world has moved on. This was about monopolising a shipping contract. Hardly altruistic idealism, and certainly little cause for moral pride. You're just a crook, plain and simple."

"You're not going to catch me out, Brooke. Just remember, we won. We outsmarted the great Isambard Kingdom Brunel. His scheme would have worked, you know, had we let it. But it didn't. It was abandoned, undersubscribed. Imagine! It's all about who you know."

"We?" asked Brooke, now intrigued, "we?"

Miss Appleby cut in viciously: "You've said quite enough, Thomas. Shut up."

"Why, it doesn't matter, Victoria. He's a dead man anyway ..."

"And Nathaniel Bellinger?" asked Brooke, "what about him?"

"Ah yes, Bellinger. Well, he got wise to things - a little too close to the truth. He had rather inconveniently overheard a conversation I had at the American Consulate in Bristol with a group of American financiers and merchants. I'm afraid he had to be eliminated before he could cause problems to our project. We've been expecting a visit from somebody since Arbuthnott announced your death a few days ago. We knew you hadn't died."

"THAT IS ENOUGH, THOMAS!" Miss Appleby shouted at her brother, "just do it! For God's sake! Kill him!" She started to walk away: tap, tap, tap from her walking cane.

Brooke casually put his hand into his trouser pocket and felt for the reassuring contours of the knuckleduster. "Go ahead," said Brooke, just as casually as he could, "but you'll have two bodies here at Newton Meadows to explain; our return to Box railway station is expected. We are awaited by a magistrate and a militia - be assured of this."

He was bluffing of course.

"You have now added the killing of a former British Army officer to your treasonable crimes. So, without our safe return ... it's your choice Appleby, and she can't run anywhere. What will you do, leave her to face the full weight of the law?"

The Applebys said nothing. Was he bluffing or not? Could there be a militia? It was possible, for Brunel had a great deal of influence across the country; particularly here in Box as it had been vital to the completion of the London to Bristol line for the Great Western Railway.

"Get the papers and go, Thomas!" shouted Miss Appleby. "Go, I can stay here. He wouldn't harm a lady, an invalid; he's far too English and honourable, aren't you, Mr Brooke? So honourable it would seem, it cost you your commission, or so I overheard at Blackfriars. You should have walked away from that unfortunate incident; allowed your superior to beat his wife, if that's what he desired." Her laugh bordered on hysterics.

"Because that's what you would have done," said Brooke, "walked away?"

He changed position so he was now directly opposite Appleby with Miss Appleby to his left side, which was just where he wanted her.

Brooke suddenly darted to one side, plunged his hand into his pocket, feeling the knuckleduster. Appleby quickly re-cocked the hammer, firing a shot at Brooke. The bullet brushed Brooke's left arm, tearing through cloth and skin. Brooke reeled. The sound again was colossal and the smoke thick, Appleby had seemingly vanished from sight. Brooke turned through three hundred and sixty degrees. He could not see Appleby. Brooke clutched hold of the knuckleduster, he was breathing fast. There amid the swirling smoke, Appleby, with a two-handed grip on the Colt, had it pointed directly at Brooke. Sight of the knuckleduster momentarily confused Appleby. Such an unexpected and yet somehow familiar piece of primitive weaponry.

A split second.

Brooke drew his arm back, hurling the duster directly at Appleby's face, with all of the force he could muster. It soared through the air, missing its intended target by a fraction of an inch.

"It's over, Brooke!" Appleby laughed. He re-cocked the hammer and discharged another round. Miss Appleby screamed for this to stop, Brooke scrambled away towards the door. Think, think, he desperately tried to recall what had happened when he and Bishop had first entered the room. The yawning, no, the snoring. Appleby had been waiting for them all along and fallen asleep in front of the fire, he'd been maintaining a vigil. The snoring, then that metallic click of the pistol and then the voice: where had they come from?

Brooke mentally retraced events, thinking rapidly and methodically.

Appleby had appeared as if out of thin air, near to the couch.

Brooke dived towards the couch, rolled and found the other Colt revolver, cocked the hammer, stood and composed himself.

And there was Appleby, appearing out of nowhere once again. Appleby raised his weapon, but this time Brooke was ready for him, Appleby was not anticipating Brooke.

Brooke's bullet caught Appleby in the left shoulder, just as Appleby's had done to Bishop.

Thomas Appleby dropped to his knees in a state of fatal shock, clutching at his chest.

Miss Appleby called out as the horror unfolded, "Thomas! Thomas!"

But she knew it was no use, a large pool of blood had already oozed from the military tunic, Appleby's body jerked in spasm; his final death throes.

Miss Appleby approached the stricken Thomas, staring down at him, drained of emotion from the cold realisation of her immediate vulnerability.

She turned to Brooke, her eyes wild, aware that this particular re-enactment of the revolutionary war was now over: "What now Mr Brooke?" she asked him.

Brooke cast a glance towards Bishop's body: "Give me the Portbury Pier share certificates and everything else that Charles either stole, or copied, from Duke Street. And I mean everything."

Miss Appleby shuffled across the room to a large desk; the tap, tap, tap of her walking cane. Her manner somehow accentuated her disability and implied that she deserved pity.

"No need to play the victim with me, Miss Appleby. It won't work. Your betrayal has caused problems and pain for too many others. You knew exactly what you were doing through your duplicity at Blackfriars."

She rummaged through the drawers frantically. "They're in here somewhere," she said, her voice now quivering.

"Why did you do it? Betray Blackfriars? Arbuthnott? Brunel? The national interest was at risk because of that betrayal."

"BECAUSE I HAD TO!" she shouted, "Crown's consortium gave me no option, they knew I was considered to be beyond reproach, and they used this. They threatened and bled the family dry in America, and then exploited Thomas to control my usefulness. Thomas was already involved in shipping and had been coerced into a poor investment in their transatlantic enterprise.

And he was foolish enough to think he was still fighting a war with the British. The consortium desperately needed that mail contract and wanted to monopolise the trade route, no matter what. This was a game with very high stakes, with too much money being risked, and the banks had already overplayed their hand with Congress. They also needed that subsidy from Congress or they'd have been sunk without trace. Profits are all that Crown Brothers understand. They have secretly organised a cartel in New York to control these routes and all that entails, and they will stop at nothing to achieve this."

Brooke was listening, absorbing every word; but pretending not to.

"Bishop lies there, dead," he said coldly, "and that is upon the hands of your brother. Just give me those papers."

Brooke threw the weapon down and went to the desk, where she held a collection of share certificates, structural drawings, tender documents and capital finance estimates, covering any number of projects. There were British Admiralty documents, reports of sea trials. From a concealed panel on the desk she produced drawings of propeller blades and engine parts for the SS Great Britain. There was even a recent copy of the Illustrated London News - Brooke took everything. He checked through them in sheer disbelief at the audacity of his enemy, He then rifled the rest of the drawers: "Is this it? Is everything here?"

"Yes."

"Is that the entire truth? No loose ends? Nobody else here involved?" Brooke was aware that he was breathing heavily.

"No. Nobody else, we didn't need anybody else, we were in complete control, on that, you have my word," she said, in an attempt at humility.

"Well now, that is particularly reassuring, Miss Appleby," with that he turned away from her, making his way to the inert body of Bishop, gently touching an arm, privately whispering, "Goodbye, Peter, for I am the one who will be forever sorry."

Brooke strode through the redolent cordite smoke and picked up the Lafayette pendant from the table. He weighed it in his hand, waiting for a response.

"NO! NO! Please don't take that … PLEASE!" she shrieked.

"No? And tell me why not? It's not going to be of use to your brother any longer, and it certainly will not save you from the gallows."

He thrust it into his pocket and shot her a rapier-like glance.

Her eyes had widened in terror: "Gallows?"

"Treason, espionage, whichever way you look at it, you will undoubtedly hang," he concluded with all the spite and emphasis he could muster.

Brooke fled the tableau of death, running across the grounds of the house. Suddenly three men appeared, out of nowhere, all carrying large bore shotguns. Appleby's watchers.

"Stop!" One of them shouted, pointing the shotgun at him, "we thought there were two of you?"

They moved closer.

Brooke did as he was bid, little choice: "There were. Appleby killed my colleague. Captain Bishop, an Army officer. Treasonable offence. He'll hang for it, rest assured." He was panting with exhaustion and emotion; and hoping his lie would work.

"What?" said one of the men, he seemed to be the senior of the three.

"The Militia are on their way from Box," Brooke took out his pocket watch as if confirming a rendezvous, "they'll be here in minutes. Through the tunnel on horseback. Like us."

The senior man nodded, recognising that they'd been outmanoeuvred: "Militia?"

"Yes and armed." With that Brooke turned and ran, praying that the watchers would do the same.

They did.

As Brooke neared the bridle path he could see the two horses. With them were Pillinger and O'Leary, still oblivious to the confrontation that had occurred inside Newton Meadows House. Behind him, in the increasing distance, the familiar crack of one final gunshot rang out across the pastureland.

It wasn't the watchers. It was another suicide in the Appleby family. And somehow, he couldn't suppress his personal satisfaction, for he was the sole survivor, and the only witness to what had just passed. Brooke felt for the silver trophy inside the safety of his pocket, the bundle of papers and documents was secure in a leather satchel; the searing pain from the wound to his arm had begun to overcome the adrenaline-charged events at Newton Meadows.

15 THE ROYAL WESTERN HOTEL

Bristol

Pillinger led at a fast gallop to Box railway station so the despondent Brooke could catch the London to Bristol mail train which was due shortly. The journey to Bristol was one of melancholy and abject regret. Peter Bishop's death was shocking as it had been completely unanticipated. Brooke was deeply immersed in a new predicament. What might now lie ahead of him? There had been no magistrate or militia, no authority of the law.

Could he have saved Bishop? Could they have known more and better planned a strategy for their visit to Newton Meadows? These were questions that would forever haunt Brooke.

Timing had been key - they had to depend upon the element of surprise. Appleby had been ready for them. He had anticipated exactly what might occur, but not the timing or the method. He kicked himself for not anticipating 'the watchers'. Of course Appleby would have spies.

Brooke visited the hotel's spa baths for an hour for further reflection. He had made his arrival known to Mrs. McCready and described the turn of events to her and the fate that had befallen Peter Bishop at Box. He would need to compose himself, to gather his thoughts before the necessary debrief that would be required with the Chief. She said she would send word immediately to the dockyard offices.

Following Mrs. McCready's usual coded tattoo, four rapid taps, Brunel responded in his usual manner.

"COME!"

"Mr Brooke, sir," she stumbled over the formality of the words, ushering Brooke into Brunel's lounge.

"Thank you, Mrs. M. Please, come in, Harry."

Brunel's tone and mood were sombre as they shook hands in a formal way, he seemingly ignored the swathe of papers Brooke had under his arm.

Brunel paused and looked him in the eye:

"Harry, I can't tell you how shocked I am to hear of ... la mort du Capitaine Bishop ..." It was an uncharacteristic response and demonstrated his genuine sorrow. Brooke was very touched at these words.

"Thank you, Isambard. I'm utterly devastated. Thomas Appleby would stop at nothing and it could only have ever ended in death, he would not allow himself to be taken alive. Bishop knew this, and in trying to create a diversion, he put himself in the gravest of positions. After everything we have ever faced, surviving the North West Frontier and Afghanistan, that he should die here now, in England, in a sleepy little hamlet..."

Brunel could feel Brooke's sorrow, sharing in the cruel irony of the situation. "I have arranged an unscheduled train to Box with the constabulary and two agents from my inner circle; they can be trusted implicitly. They will be there now, as we speak. Rest assured, Harry, everything will be secured and all necessary arrangements made, I will attend to this personally. This ... this incident must not become public knowledge."

"No, I understand."

"Now," said Brunel, "what exactly did you find in the way of evidence?"

Brooke wandered towards Brunel's drawing board, carefully depositing the documents onto it, naming each piece as he did so:

"I believe we have discovered enough evidence: the share certificates for the Portbury Pier and Railway Company, in your name, Mr Guppy's and Mr Wainwright's, eighty thousand pounds' worth in total. Plus, there is another one hundred and twenty thousand pounds' worth in other people's names, some of which I recognise from our conversations. There are also many Admiralty papers, reports and designs; I took a look through the material on my way back to Bristol. I hope you don't mind, I wanted to get a measure of Appleby's penetration of your business interests."

Brunel was flabbergasted by Brooke's revelations: "My God, Harry. This has been far worse than I had ever imagined; passing this information over to our American competitors. Quite extraordinary; they knew exactly what we were doing, our every move."

"Yes, and the certificates stolen from your London residence, by one Charles Appleby, the son of our arch-villain Thomas. Charles was also nephew of the treacherous Miss Appleby ... and ..."

"The Swindon assailant. Guppy was right then, Appleby was our man." Brunel sifted through the papers: "The propeller designed by Francis Smith, yes, we ran tests on these here, with Guppy and Arbuthnott, of course."

"And there are these assorted drawings," Brooke continued, "exact copies made by the errant Charles ... the Clifton Bridge here, the Hungerford Bridge, Balmoral Bridge, the Bristol railway station and even the Portbury Pier and Railway."

"Quite unbelievable," said Brunel, looking at each document in utter disbelief, "they are exactly as my originals."

"Yes, and reproduced from his memory, that's why there was nothing actually missing from your house, apart from the shares - documents merely re-arranged, so to speak. So, it is a mission accomplished ..."

"But not without cost," Brunel summed up solemnly.

"No, sir, not without cost," Brooke agreed, "and I discovered something else, purely by chance."

"Oh really, and what was that?"

"Nathaniel Bellinger was murdered by Charles Appleby."

"Nathaniel? Murdered?" another shocking revelation for Brunel to absorb.

"I recall Peter mentioning having seen a newspaper headline, something like, 'Merchant is found murdered in Bloomsbury'. It seemed like too much of a coincidence. Charles Appleby was staying at the Russell Square Hotel and the body of a man, who just happened to be part of your inner circle, was found near to that location. Thomas Appleby confirmed the details to me."

"They admitted this?" asked Brunel, amazed.

"Yes, without too much detail; Bellinger had overheard a conversation at the American Consulate, here in Bristol. Once he began to ask leading questions, he had to be silenced."

"I'll notify the authorities; they can contact Nathaniel's wife and family."

"Yes, but there's no evidence and no perpetrator to charge, They're all dead."

As he was sifting through these papers, Brunel stumbled upon an opened copy of the Illustrated London News. Something on the page which someone had ringed with pencil captured his attention, he looked at it. He put it down amongst all the other documents. Brooke could just about see an advertisement and two words struck him: 'Cooper Watts'. He wondered what they could possibly signify.

"There was another thing, Isambard."

"Oh?"

"Miss Appleby mentioned Crown Brothers; it's a New York bank, financiers. Ruthless in their pursuit of financial power and profits, they have organised some kind of secretive cartel to monopolise the transatlantic route. She said they were based in New York and it sounded significant, if it's true. They have some controlling interest in every operating line. They control the competition, so that there can be no competition. Ego and greed."

"Unless it was a trick of some kind; a ploy, what do you think?" Brunel chose his words carefully and was deep in thought.

"I don't think so; in view of what she was just about to do, she didn't need to divulge the precise details."

Brunel rubbed his chin: "That's true enough. I'll get Cornelius to look into it. In fact, Harry, this might require some deeper consideration."

He beckoned: "Please come, sit with me a while, Harry. We need to talk further, Sit down, please."

"Thank you."

Brooke waited, sensing somehow that there might be more

trouble in store.

"You've done a good job here, Harry, you couldn't have done better. But the fate of Captain Bishop and the deaths of those two key figures at Newton Meadows mean we will have to make immediate plans. Now. Today. For when the constables return, they will undoubtedly ask questions requiring answers. Cornelius can help, but we need to formulate a plan. Now."

"I see," Brooke was apprehensive.

"I admit, I had anticipated some grievous outcome to this affair, but not so ... well ... tragic."

Brunel rose and went to a chest of drawers. Pulling one open, he removed a thick manila envelope upon which was embossed the Great Western Railway emblem. He continued his rhetoric: "There is one thousand pounds in this envelope, Harry, you will obtain rail tickets for Liverpool, via London, from Bristol."

Brooke interjected for, despite the generous offer, he had other questions on his mind. "I don't like the sound of this Isambard ... I have to ..."

But Brunel countered: "Just hear me out, Harry, please just listen to what I have to say. And, a first-class ticket to Melbourne, on the SS Great Britain; it will be her inaugural voyage to Australia."

Brooke's disappointment was obvious: One Single Ticket. How significant that sounded now. And how portentous.

"So, I am to become a fugitive, is this how it all ends then?" he said, with a trace of resentfulness towards Brunel.

"I would rather think of it as a beginning than an end, Harry, with a chance for a fresh start in life - one that you know only too well you will need. It is an opportunity, and another idea has just occurred to me also."

"And Miss Louiseau?" Brooke enquired, in an attempt to bring the meeting around to more pleasing thoughts and searching for common ground with Brunel.

"Isabelle?" was Brunel's questioning reply, "why, she's at the music school, her piano exam is today, if you recall? There is a certain grade or standard which she has to achieve, in order to return to the conservatoire in Paris, to continue her studies."

"Ah yes, of course, the Conservatoire de Paris." Brooke could hear her saying those words as he recalled their first encounter in the hotel. But in a few days the world had moved on, yet again.

"Do you recall the detail of our first meeting, Harry, here in this room?"

"Yes, I was just thinking about it. You beat the hearth with that steel poker, frightening Miss Louiseau."

"Ah yes, the falling ember. But not that. I told you that nothing is impossible and that from that time you were working for me, do you not remember that?"

"Yes, of course I do."

"I knew then that you could be my right-hand man, and that is still very much the case, even though circumstances have changed rather drastically. What do you think?"

"That I should be on my way to the railway station?" said Harry with some compliance.

"Yes, but the SS Great Britain does not sail for Australia until the 21st of August, four months hence. That gives us four months!"

"Four months?" asked Brooke, confused, "to do what, exactly?"

"Why, to finally complete the mission on which you have embarked, Harry; to solve the puzzle. You said but a few moments ago that Miss Appleby had specifically mentioned Crown Brothers, and that they are behind some kind of ruthless cartel based in New York, or words to that effect."

Brooke was amazed once again by Brunel's thought pattern: "Are you suggesting that I travel to America?"

"Why not? You have four months in which to make a round trip, the shipping timetables will allow for it and you might just discover the truth of the matter. Were the Applebys acting alone, or were they the instruments of others, as claimed by Miss Appleby? Who has established this cartel? There is only one way to find out, and you are the very man to do it."

Brooke couldn't fail to appreciate of Brunel's adeptness of thought, his face formed a wry smile: "If you put it like that, I have very little choice in the matter."

"Do you want a choice, Harry?" Brunel arched an eyebrow and scribbled down an address on a piece of paper, handing it to Brooke.

"This is the address for Cornelius Arbuthnott in Richmond Hill. I want you to go there immediately and await further instructions. Is that clear? It is most important that you and he have a discussion."

"Alright, if you say so," said Brooke, suspecting Brunel already had some kind of contingency plan.

"You cannot afford to remain here a moment longer."

"I understand." A flat acceptance of the situation that had been outlined by the great man.

"Have faith, Harry, always have faith, you'll see," said Brunel, in an attempt to reassure Brooke.

Brooke looked at him doubtfully. "Faith? Are you really sure about that Isambard, really?"

"Yes. Faith gives substance to our hopes and makes us certain of realities we do not see - it's a verse from the book of Hebrews; in the Bible."

Brooke would not dispute this quotation from the Bible.

"I'll see to everything here in Bristol and Box. I will not let you down," said Brunel, with an air of finality.

They shook hands as comrades, a fond but apprehensive farewell, Brunel left the room, closing the door softly behind him.

Brooke sank into his armchair reflecting on the discussion, aware that Isabelle had barely figured in any of the conversation that had occurred between him and Brunel. His heart ached for the loss of Bishop, and what now appeared to be his imminent separation from Isabelle.

As his final act here, Brooke sat at Brunel's desk, writing a brief note. He slipped it inside a standard blue company envelope, dropped in the Lafayette pendant, applying a wax seal.

He'd simply addressed it 'ISAMBARD'.

16 THE JOURNEY TO LONDON

Harry Brooke sat alone in his compartment, gazing haphazardly out of the window as the train pulled away from the platform at Bristol Terminus Station 'on the up' to Paddington. His spirits had never seemed lower, his present thoughts were of Peter Bishop who, in the worst of circumstances, could be the irrepressible optimist. Bishop had lifted Brooke's spirits and been a constant source of encouragement - almost as if it were his role to play in Brooke's life, expecting very little from anything in his own.

Bishop had faced Appleby and confronted him with the bitter truth of his son's suicide, and it had cost him his life. But why on earth hadn't Peter shown him that blessed drawing? Was it a lack of time, or opportunity, or, was it some other reason? Did Bishop want to prove that he could take on a task without being directly asked or instructed? He was, after all, viewed by many as being

Brooke's side man.

Brooke would never know the answer to this. He closed his eyes and let his mind wander; the insistent beat of the rails led him to a state of meditation.

A stream of images crept into his mind …

The day before the ill-fated visit to Newton Meadows, following the revelations offered by Bishop's sketch and the adoption of a weak strategy, Brooke had been given leave by Dr Hartland to take some air on Durdham Down. This place had intrigued Brooke, it is a large expanse of open grass parkland offering views out towards Somerset in one direction, the Avon Gorge in another, and in the far distance, the hills of Wales. But he could also gaze down into the gorge, seeing the route of the River Avon between the Bristol Channel and the city docks. He now clearly understood the need for Brunel's Portbury Pier and Railway scheme.

Brooke had taken the air with Isabelle, with Mrs. McCready as her chaperone. Brunel had made the splendid and pragmatic suggestion that Peter Bishop should join them to balance the group. They had enjoyed a splendid spring day, blue skies and sunshine had blessed the occasion - it was an absolute tonic. Pillinger, had decked out the carriage with a seasonal floral decoration, and chosen a steady, circuitous route from the house in Cornwallis Crescent that would elevate them gradually, by way of Clifton village, crossing Clifton Down, eventually reaching Durdham Down where horse races were scheduled for that day, a cause of much excitement.

Pillinger delivered the group to a location known as Cook's Folly, where they might be lucky enough to get grandstand seating. Bishop and Mrs. M had gone to the paddock area to view the horses at close quarters. Pillinger had other coachmen with whom he could engage in comparative gossip. Brooke had seized upon this singular opportunity to have a moment alone with Isabelle, and they found themselves a quieter spot away from the hurly-burly of the carnival atmosphere, maintaining their privacy by the deft use of a parasol.

The train jolted to a halt. Brooke opened one eye and saw that it had arrived at Bath Spa railway station. His contemplation was disturbed by a loud hiss and human commotion outside his compartment cocoon. He closed his eyes and was instantly back on the Downs in Bristol.

"Most of the relatively few women that I have encountered during my brief visit to Bristol seem to resent me," he said to Isabelle, "especially that crone I met at the music school."

Isabelle had smiled at this, taking a little time before answering.

She was composing her words with care, her eyes failing to meet his as she struggled to find words.

"It's not you they resent, Harry, it's me. All, with the exception of Mrs. M, but even she was dubious about me to begin with."

"Oh really?"

"Because," another pause for thought and consideration, "because I am French, Roman Catholic, unmarried and ..."

"Attractive?" Brooke interjected, because it was only too obvious to him, she had made other women jealous through her freedom of spirit - although she was clearly very loath to say this herself.

"I suppose so, yes, maybe. I can't help my appearance or the place of my birth. But, the fact that I am not married and therefore not dutiful makes my virtue questionable - to them. Yes, they are suspicious of me."

"That's ridiculous, jealous, more likely." Brooke had taken out a cigarette, placing it in his ivory holder, as he always did.

She watched him carefully.

"It's true. I don't conform to their way of thinking ... their petty values. What do you call it ... of establishment?"

"The establishment, I believe is what they call it," he ventured with due caution and a trace of amusement.

"Yes, and the way they conduct their lives, especially that old viper you mentioned at the music school! The first time I met her, I had gone there to play - I removed my gloves, there is no engagement ring upon my finger, it brought her instant disapproval of me!"

Brooke grinned as she continued.

"But it's very similar in France, especially around the family home in Normandy and in Parisian society. Yes, I am twenty-three years old and probably should be married to a husband who works in finance - we should already have two children and live in a house in the suburbs. I should be content with that sort of life and it would be my duty to supervise this domestic scene. Instead ..."

"Instead, you are travelling, you are still learning because you are meeting many people."

Isabelle blushed, so he continued quickly, "Very admirable, Isabelle, I see your choices as being cultured. One day, such an attitude may be commonplace amongst all women - these female attitudes now are simply due to jealousy of your free spirit, that is all."

"Maybe," she bit her bottom lip, it was a tiny coquettish mannerism.

"Yes!"

Isabelle had been very surprised at Brooke's relaxed view of her lifestyle. His accepting attitude was similar to that of her uncle, which was what enabled her to enjoy such a playful relationship with Brunel. Brooke had clearly seen inside this relationship; it had given him an insight to both their characters. Isabelle's hand shot to her mouth as she now laughed aloud, embarrassed. It was infectious - they were both reduced to fits of hilarity.

The train jolted to another halt. Brooke opened an eye to look outside. He found himself looking at Swindon railway station and Rigby's Hotel - the scene of his recent altercation, but oh, how the world had changed since. Once again he became aware of the billowing steam and the human commotion upon the platform.

"Swindon break! Ten minutes!" shouted the guard, passing by Brooke's compartment and looking within, calling, "Refreshments!"

Did the guard take a second look at him?

Was there a glimmer of recognition in that glance? … hopefully not.

Brooke closed his eyes, pulled up his collar in an attempt at concealment and returned again to his private theatre of scenarios.

"And what of you, Mr Brooke?" Isabelle had asked him: "You are a bit of a mystery, are you not?"

"Not really, I'm just an old soldier."

"Oh, but you are, sir!" she mocked, in imitation of an upper-class English accent. "Pleasingly so, particularly today, sir. Finely attired in your suit, waistcoat and tie - especially for the races. But, there is something else about you, isn't there, Mr Brooke?"

"Such as?" he asked, disarmed by her subtle stroking of his vanity.

"You do … what was Captain Bishop's expression; get into scrapes? I did not know what this expression alluded to … scrapes

... I had to ask Mrs. M."

She had become serious once again - feigning to look away, she shot him a probing question.

"Has there ever been anyone in your life, Mr Brooke ... never someone special?"

Now it was his turn to look away, suddenly distant. Was he considering the question, or a suitable answer?

"Forgive me, for I have intruded ... I am sorry, I can see by your face."

"No, no, it's quite all right, Isabelle, only this is neither the right time nor place."

"We will find the right time and the right place, Mr Brooke. I think it will be so. I think destiny has intervened."

She touched him, an innocent gesture, yet in that moment, it was the most enduringly intimate gesture he had experienced.

He shivered now at the recollection of that moment, quite innocent, but so compelling.

Her face ... vanished. Whatever she was about to say was lost forever.

"There you are!" roared Bishop, bounding into the scene with unbridled enthusiasm: "Did you not see the last race? We won! Look! Mrs. M must be my lucky charm!"

Mrs. M revealed a handful of silver coins: "That's a first for me, I can tell you," she exclaimed.

Isabelle smiled, looked away, distracted by something. A roar had gone up from the grandstand.

"Come on, Harry, let's take a libation, I am disposed to place another wager. What say you, Miss Louiseau? Oh, do come on!"

The cheering and jollity drew them in like moths to a flame.

The train slowed and shuddered to a final stop. Brooke once again opened a cautious eye and looked out of the carriage window. Paddington railway station, a mist of swirling steam, populated by hurrying porters and passengers, families with their domestic retinue. Everybody trying to get somewhere. Harry Brooke took out the piece of paper bearing Arbuthnott's address and considered the four-month hiatus ahead of him - what had Brunel been thinking?

Rising from his seat, he stretched, placing the series of dreams in an appropriate place within his mind, somewhere distant from his present attentions. He mused on how real some dreams can seem, somehow, so tactile. He gathered up his belongings, opened the compartment door, alighting to the platform and disappearing among the denizens of the capital's populace. So now to find Arbuthnott. The first leg of his shadowy enforced journey was complete.

17 ARBUTHNOTT'S RETREAT IN RICHMOND HILL

April 1852

Cornelius Arbuthnott's retreat in Richmond Hill was not unlike the man himself: an elegant façade, well built and full of surprises.

The carriage dropped Brooke outside the front door, and he tipped the driver handsomely. It had been an amusing journey from Paddington, a fast chase through the narrow cobbled streets and thoroughfares of south-west London to the lush green fields of Surrey. The man was chatty, his news of London gossip, recent fares and foreign policy covered a myriad of subjects in the hour-long journey. Brooke said little, happy to listen and let his mind wander. To his surprise, the front door opened just as he was about to knock. Arbuthnott stood there as large as life, beaming and wearing evening dress. Brooke could hear animated voices from within the house, the music of a string quartet and the sound of clinking glasses. Arbuthnott did not appear surprised to see Brooke, and ushered him in cordially. There was a sudden shriek of laughter and Brooke fancied the musicians may have missed a beat.

"Mr Brooke, do come in. Leave your trunk by the hat stand, the staff will attend to it shortly.

"Am I intruding?" Brooke felt vaguely embarrassed.

"Not at all. I've been expecting you. I just didn't know when. But I caught sight of your carriage as I was passing the drawing room window."

Once inside, Brooke inclined his head towards the room from which the sounds of the party were emanating through open neo-classical double doors. "A celebration of some kind?" he asked.

"My wife Arianna's significant birthday. Although I dare not reveal exactly how significant. Suffice it to say that she's been planning it for months. Invitations, food, wine, music, her dress. So much for her to … delegate … poor lamb." He smiled at his own joke.

"I hope she's sure my arrival isn't too inconvenient."

"Quite sure." Arbuthnott led Brooke across a marble tiled hallway into an adjacent room, from which a dull light emitted. The spacious hallway was adorned with pots of plants: cacti, bromelia, polyscias, and roses. It resembled a well-stocked conservatory. As Arbuthnott was about to close the door, a woman's voice called coquettishly, "Don't be too long Buttie. Aunt Agatha is anxious to deliver her amusing speech. Oh, and your guest's luggage has been taken upstairs. He's in the Ivy Suite."

Buttie! Brooke grinned. The man-at-home was a far cry from his image at the stuffy offices at Blackfriars or the formality of Brunel's hotel in Bristol. Arbuthnott closed the door and turned the lamps up. To Brooke's surprise, the room was a very extensive library with polished oak shelves lined with leather-bound tomes, and oil paintings on some of the walls. These were mainly portraits of severe-looking men in military uniform. The closed drapes hung from ceiling to floor, and Brooke could imagine sweeping lawns beyond the Regency windows. This was clearly a very substantial country pile, similar in size and opulence to Newton Meadows; the sort of retreat that had manicured borders and a team of gardeners.

"Sherry?" asked Arbuthnott with a smile as he caught Brooke looking at a particular oil painting.

"Thank you."

"Oh, don't mind those stern old faces; noble patricians of the family's past. Almost a dynasty in this part of Surrey. The Arbuthnotts go back a long way – military - political – ecclesiastical; the law, of course, and farming. We have about five hundred acres here. Yes, the family has lived in this house for, what, over two hundred years?" Arbuthnott sauntered over to a substantial oak dresser and poured two generous measures of Amontillado into crystal glasses. There were other decanters of, presumably, cognac, whisky and port on a silver salver. Brooke took the proffered glass and was beckoned to sit in one of several leather armchairs. Arbuthnott made himself comfortable in another. He filled his pipe from a battered old oilskin tobacco pouch, lit the bowl enthusiastically and was immediately engulfed in a cloud of blue smoke. He sipped his sherry reflectively. Was the routine all a ploy to gain time in which to compose and consider his thoughts? "Do you remember, Mr Brooke, when we first met in the dining room at Paddington? I cautioned you about the existence of dark forces?"

"Yes."

"You were dismissive of the notion?" Arbuthnott sucked on the stem of his pipe with fervour and obvious enjoyment.

"Not dismissive, just cautious. I was surprised, that's all."

Arbuthnott suddenly drained his glass and placed it on a small card table beside him: "Tell me what happened at Box. And then we can discuss your forthcoming trip to America, and its ultimate purpose."

So, Arbuthnott knew about the plan. And yet, how could he?

Brooke omitted nothing as he recounted his story, and found the revelation cathartic in an unintended way. The initial encounter with Appleby, his murder of Captain Bishop, Miss Appleby's suicide, the recovery of the stolen documents and certificates, his escape from Appleby's watchers. He left no detail out. Twice the library door was knocked upon; and twice Arbuthnott responded with 'not now'. They had replenished their glasses several times, the decanter was now visibly depleted. Arbuthnott's facial expressions metamorphosed from shock to puzzlement as

Brooke's tale concluded with the discussion he'd had with Brunel earlier that day in Bristol. Arbuthnott said nothing during this lengthy disclosure, save the odd sigh or expletive. Finally he stood and went over to his desk upon which lay an open copy of the Illustrated London News; his tone was solemn.

"Two days before Nathaniel Bellinger was murdered, he gave me two copies of this. We'd arranged to meet again in Bloomsbury to discuss this advertisement further." Arbuthnott was about to hand the paper over to Brooke, but stopped as if a further thought occurred to him. "When Captain Bishop's drawing revealed the face – eventually – of Thomas Appleby, everything became clearer. Let's say it certainly explained why Nathaniel desired a further meeting." Arbuthnott finally handed Brooke the opened paper. "It may be part of the reason why he was killed."

"Isambard had a copy of this in Bristol," said Brooke, as he took the paper.

Arbuthnott sucked his pipe and smiled: "Isambard had the other copy. Note the date, if you please Mr Brooke - 21st February 1852.

FOR THE WEEK ENDING
21ST FEBRUARY 1852

COOPER WATTS

ADVANCE ANNOUNCEMENT.

YACHT FOR SALE - AT AUCTION.

To be held at the NEW YORK PAVILION, WALL STREET, NEW YORK. 3rd June 1852.

Class and type: Gaff schooner (built 1847, Boston).

Tonnage: 100.   Length: LOA 100'.
Beam: 22' 10".   Draught: 10' 11".
Propulsion: Sail.
Construction: Hull material, wood; white oak, locust cedar and chestnut.

WILLIAM APPLEBY SHIPPING COMPANY

is happy to offer this unique gaff schooner for sale at auction, designed by James Stevens, Esq.

The vessel is fast, seaworthy and suitable for competition.

A traditional 'cod head and mackerel tail' design, built in Boston, Massachusetts.

Maiden voyage (chartered): New Haven - New York - Philadelphia - Savannah - Jacksonville and return.

Second voyage: to Lisbon, Portugal and return.

Arbuthnott's expression was grim: "The competition for the Atlantic route is ruthless; the rewards bountiful, as we all know …" he paused and gazed at the image of one of Brooke finished reading and said: "According to Miss Appleby, the Crown Brothers in New York exerted considerable leverage: 'they threatened and bled the family dry in America' were her exact words. And I have to say, I believed her. As I said to Isambard, she had no reason to lie. Particularly in view of what happened moments later."

"She took her own life."

"Yes, for her there was little other option."

Brooke sensed that there was a lot more to come, and waited. He lit one of his hand-rolled cigarettes and inhaled deeply, savouring the flavour. "What exactly is it you want from me, Cornelius? I face the prospect of an all-expenses-paid trip to America; that much was clear from Isambard. But why exactly am I here in Surrey when I could have gone directly to Liverpool and boarded the ship?"

Arbuthnott returned to his chair, picked up his glass and was disappointed to find it empty. "You'll stay here tonight, Harry and depart in the morning after a hearty country breakfast. My driver, Thomas, will take you to the station; then you'll take the train as agreed. There is much to do."

"Thank you. I confess the thought of a comfortable bed before a long voyage consoles me. But, with respect, you have still not answered my question."

There was a further knock at the door. Arbuthnott responded with, "Five minutes," a tad frostily. The response amused Brooke; presumably it was Arbuthnott's wife knocking, and after all, it was her birthday party.

"The truth is what we seek, Harry. We need to discover whether this duplicitous scheme against Mr Brunel is an authorised, sanctioned piece of American government policy; or merely the will of common thieves."

Brooke raised his eyebrows: "We?"

"I have two hats; one is my role as a lawyer at Blackfriars, the other is within a secret British government department. Officially, in that capacity, I work for the Foreign Office. In fact, I answer directly to the Prime Minister. And to Mr Brunel, of course." He sniggered. Was it a joke?

Brooke puffed out his cheeks with a sigh: "I see."

"I don't need to tell you that this information is privileged. Not even my wife knows. It has to be that way, you see?"

"I understand, and I appreciate your candour."

Arbuthnott continued: "It is possible that the British and American administrations can both be duped by clever and resourceful players. Particularly in respect of government grants and subsidies. And particularly when the two don't seem to be able to communicate with one another effectively."

"I will do everything in my power to help, Cornelius."

"Good. You are uniquely qualified to carry out this assignment, Harry. Besides your distinguished military career, you have an informed insight into Blackfriars, Mr Brunel and the Appleby clan. If anyone can discover the truth, it is you."

As if on cue, there was a final tap upon the library door to which Arbuthnott finally replied, "Come in Arianna."

The door opened, and the most beautiful woman entered. She looked positively radiant in a long shimmering ballgown and silk gloves. She must have been twenty years Arbuthnott's junior. Her face resembled a classic portrait: slightly tanned flawless skin, perfect bone structure, delicate feminine features which were perhaps Mediterranean in origin. She had a wide, sensuous mouth, and when she smiled it gave her an air of mischief. Her brown eyes sparkled as she spoke. "You must be Harry Brooke," she said, "come and join our little soiree. Did Buttie tell you it's my birthday!"

Brooke stood courteously: "Good evening, Mrs. Arbuthnott. Yes, I believe he did mention something."

"Come Darling," she said looping her arm for her husband to take, "the speech awaits and so does your lovely champagne. A treat!"

Arbuthnott smiled conspiratorially at Brooke, then took his wife's arm and they wandered out together towards the party. Brooke pocketed his silver cigarette case and finished his drink. So, he thought to himself, Cornelius Arbuthnott is some manner of government spy supremo, answerable to the PM. Suddenly the stakes were much higher, and he had been trusted. This was a far cry from the British Army in Afghanistan or the rooftops of Belgravia. Peter would be proud of him. And so would Isabelle.

Arianna turned briefly and smiled, "Quickly; or you'll miss the speech!"

"All right," said Brooke, "on my way."

Yes, he thought to himself, Arbuthnott was full of surprises. Whatever next?

18 NEW YORK CITY

14th May 1852

After a turbulent two-week journey across the Atlantic, Harry Brooke disembarked from the SS Great Britain. He breathed in the air of the city, together with hordes of others, mainly European immigrants. How delightful it was to be still at last; although he still felt the motion of the ship, something he never got used to. He glanced up at the sun; had he gone back in time, or was he out of sorts? Like his fellow passengers he was weary and unsure about his future. The meeting with Arbuthnott had been long and thorough - a key point of the discussion had been the auction announcement, then obviously the tactics and strategy for Brooke's emplacement in New York. The steamship timetables were a critical factor, as timing was crucial. Brooke was booked on the inaugural sailing of the SS Great Britain to Australia, so he had to be in Liverpool by the time it was due to depart on the twenty-first of August. The ship was scheduled to depart from New York on the fifth of June, so he had ample time to go about his business. Ultimately, he knew he would have to play this by ear, venturing into the unknown with no real plan, it was the nature of his life. He would survive by instinct; there was no other option. The morning at Newton Meadows had all but drained him, but the revelations there had provided the impetus to go on, to give substance to Bishop's sacrifice.

Walking down the ship's gang plank, Brooke didn't need that copy of the Illustrated London News - he'd memorised every word. Looking around, he realised that virtually all of his fellow travellers had come in search of a new life. They would never return home. Their home would now be wherever they found it in America.

New York was bright, it was warm and almost humid. The emergent passengers struggled onto this new land with their belongings, this was probably only the beginning of another long journey, taking them somewhat beyond the bounds of the city - the new frontier.

New York had been described as 'a huge, semi-barbarous metropolis' with filthy streets and poor sanitation. To Brooke, this seemed to be quite true as he progressed from the wharf into the city. Looking around him, these immigrants looked more like survivors than pioneers. Immigrants were arriving at an average rate of a quarter of a million people per year. They had come from across Europe, there were a dozen different languages that he could hear along the wharf as he had left the ship. Each person brought something new or different to this 'new world'.

Brooke eventually found his destination, which had been recommended to him by a steward from the ship: The New York Hotel at 721 Broadway, near Washington Square Park. It was the best that Greenwich had to offer. The hotel, which opened in 1843, was located between East 8th Street and West 4th Street. Its lobby was plush, decorated with fabric and plants. Brooke had no trouble in booking a room. He was given his key and advised of the full à la carte room service menu which would be available to him. In addition, he could request a valet and a laundry facility.

He knew he had about two weeks in which to reconnoitre the

city and find his bearings before the auction on Wall Street. Understanding the geography of a place was fundamental Army practice, particularly when an unknown enemy may be lurking. The enemy had the advantage: they knew the streets. His first mission would be to change some pounds into dollars and buy a street map, if there was such a thing. If not, he would draw one. He swallowed and thought of Peter Bishop, whose forte that would have been.

19 NEW YORK CITY

3rd June 1852

The New York Pavilion was located on Wall Street, in Lower Manhattan; the Cooper-Watts Auction Room was a room within it. The building felt more like a palace than a mere pavilion - it was mainly iron and glass: standing three storeys high with a central apex, it housed galleries of shops. There was also an observatory, some five hundred feet in height, offering extensive views of Lower Manhattan, the East River, the city of Brooklyn, the Hudson River and Jersey City. Brooke felt dressed for the occasion and confidently entered the reception area. It was full of exotic and captivating culinary aromas - ah, those immigrants that hadn't ventured much farther than their disembarkation point. But it was a day out, a little entertainment, and this was quite an early start for the day's frivolities. Brooke followed the COOPER-WATTS SALE ROOM sign and roamed through the many exhibition halls. It was both marvellous and garish in equal measure. One could invest in anything it would seem. There were opportunities on offer in railroads and in shipping. This was Manhattan, the heartbeat of New York, now that the English no longer governed it.

The auction room was packed. Thirty rows of bench seats were already occupied, many people were milling around the aisles and down the sides. The focal point was the auctioneer's lectern - the auction block - and behind that, the Gaff Schooner. All one hundred feet of her, mounted upon wooden blocks, disguised by an elaborate adornment of flowers.

There was a hubbub of excitement in the air, a thrill of anticipation - but it was all about money. To the rear of the auction room was a bar - the affluent quaffed champagne. This was a far cry from the tenements and sordid dirty streets he had traversed a few days before.

Attention was drawn by the stroke of a gavel: "Fifteen minutes, please, everyone - take your seats. Please ensure you have registered if you are bidding. Fourteen minutes …!"

And then Brooke saw a face that he recognised, although it was a person he did not know.

William Appleby. He was similar in appearance to Thomas Appleby and his son, Charles, with dark eyes, sharp nose, thin lips, high forehead, replete with haughty expression. Familiar and yet …

Brooke manoeuvred himself towards this character. This particular Appleby was middle aged, probably of a similar age to the deceased Thomas, and could easily have passed as a sibling. He was well dressed in quality clothing, but he was noticeably perspiring. He looked anxious or worried. He constantly dabbed at his lips or his brow with a handkerchief.

"Why are you selling her?" asked Brooke casually, "she's a beauty, and has all of those sea trials and a solid provenance."

Appleby turned warily. "Do I know you?"

"We've met before," Brooke lied, as confidently as he could.

For a moment there was an uneasy silence. "I'm selling because I have to. I have no choice, if it's all the same to you."

In the few words of that exchange, Brooke detected a very familiar accent, but more than that he detected the man's fear.

A heftily-built man strode towards them, tipping his hat to anybody he chose.

He swayed his way through the assembled crowd like royalty,

exuding a self-confidence that bordered on arrogance.

Brooke disliked him immediately.

"Now there you are, William ... thought we'd lost you," he glanced at Brooke, "and who's this?"

Appleby looked blank and more deeply worried.

"Le Maitre," said Brooke, "Phillip Le Maitre," he offered his hand, which the big man rudely ignored.

"Bidding for the yacht?" he asked, using as few words as possible.

"No," said Brooke, irritated.

The large man looked him up and down, as a disappointed tailor might regard an ill-fitting suit.

"I thought not ... a little out of your league, I'd guess."

He turned back to Appleby.

"Come on, William, you promised to buy me a drink before the fun starts."

He grabbed Appleby's arm ushering him towards the auction room bar, leaving Brooke smarting at this intrusion.

"Two minutes!" the bang of the gavel drew attention to the arrival of the auctioneer at the podium. His appearance was something akin to that of a judge handing down a sentence of capital punishment. A bell tolled.

"Welcome everyone, to Cooper-Watts on a bright, sunny day, here in New York City.

This is our fiftieth auction at the New York Pavilion."

There was a ripple of applause across the smoke-filled room, then the hubbub died down.

"Today, we have this Gaff Schooner on offer ... designed by Mr James Stevens and built in Boston, Massachusetts ... 1847 ...y'all have your catalogues and bidding paddles ... Mr William Appleby, the vendor, is more than happy to entertain any questions from the buyer - AFTER THE SALE!"

This drew a chuckle of polite laughter, part of the auctioneer's tactic. Appleby looked away embarrassed, if not humiliated, whilst his fat acquaintance slapped him on the back with false enthusiasm.

"Now where shall we start the bidding? Who'll give me five hundred dollars?"

"Six!" A sudden quick voice and bidding paddle raised to identify the location.

"Seven!"

"Nine!"

"Thank you, Mr Rothschild!" said the auctioneer.

"Eleven hundred!"

"Twelve hundred!"

"Thank you, sir," roared the auctioneer in excitement. There was a moment's silence, then he continued. "Extensive sea trials, all the way to Europe, she's been to Portugal and back. Never sank once!"

"Two thousand dollars," another voice punctuated the tension.

"Thank you, Mr Astor. Two thousand in the room here ... any runners ...?" he looked towards the exits for any signs of messenger boys waving their 'ticket bids'.

A moment's silence, then a sip of water: theatrical thirst - a pause.

"Twenty-five hundred."

A sudden roar of excitement: "Thank you sir! Come on folks ... she's white oak, locust cedar and chestnut ... sails were made in Ireland ... ocean-going yacht."

"Three thousand."

"Thank you, Mr Morgan ... that is three thousand American dollars?" he asked, with good humour.

"Sure is," came the swift response.

"Any more?" cried the auctioneer. He needed more. He looked across at Appleby, he shook his head - three thousand was nowhere near enough.

"Mr Crown! You're very quiet today, sir! Have you just bought another boat?"

The man who had kidnapped Appleby from Brooke shook his head, all smiles and self-deprecation, played to the crowd, merely waved it away with a gesture of his hands.

But behind the outward bravado, Brooke could sense Crown's anger towards the auctioneer.

"This vessel," said the auctioneer, "has sailed to England with a crew - they're not included in today's lot, by the way."

Another wave of laughter amongst the crowd.

"She sailed around the Isle of Wight and back here to New York Harbour. Right here," he pointed his hand in the general direction of the East River and the landing wharves, just a short distance away.

"Four thousand dollars," a man called out; it sounded like an instruction.

"Thank you, Mr Rockefeller. Four thousand dollars," the auctioneer surveyed the room, biding his time, thinking of the commission.

"FOUR THOUSAND once!" he cried aloud.

"Forty-five hundred," a familiar voice; faces turned.

"Thank you again, Mr Rothschild ... for you, I can find a crew!"

More laughter, a little nervous, was it getting near the closing bid?

"Forty-five hundred dollars ... the bid now stands at forty-five hundred. Any more bids today? What can we do here?"

The auctioneer wiped his brow. What a performance! Then, complete silence - the serious bidders all looked at one another, daggers drawn. They could all afford this, for them, it was a morning's entertainment and a means of maintaining their notoriety.

An elderly Italian gentleman at the front quietly raised his bidding paddle with one hand and raised five rheumatic digits with the other.

"Five thousand dollars, thank you, Signor Bellini ... I have five thousand dollars right here in front of me. Any advance? Anybody?"

The auctioneer glanced at Appleby who shrugged as if he didn't care, it was a curious gesture and Brooke was observing him carefully.

"Five thousand? Five thousand once ... five thousand twice," he raised his gavel, about to go thrice ... then ...

"SIX!" a solitary voice, male, a new bidder.

"Six thousand dollars, thank you, Mr Vanderbilt. Six thousand dollars! Six thousand dollars I am bid for this wonderful vessel ... I can advance this five hundred to sixty-five hundred, if will help."

A sea of faces, arms folded, looked in awe around the room expectantly ...

"Six thousand dollars then ... six thousand dollars once ... six thousand dollars twice ..." a hesitation, then BANG! The gavel went down hard on the block, "SOLD at six thousand dollars! Well done, sir! She is now yours! You can sail her home!"

There was a round of applause and almost at once, people stood and were exiting the room as though their lives depended upon it.

Brooke cast a glance towards the auction room bar, Appleby and his associate had vanished. He cursed himself for looking away to watch the auction's closing proceedings.

He dashed towards the exit, brushing past people and making his apologies as he did so.

He scanned a sea of people all heading in a variety of directions - there wasn't a chance of spotting the two men in this crowd.

Brooke strolled back into the auction room, which was deserted but for a few remaining stragglers. The auctioneer was standing at the bar drinking a large beer. Brooke wandered over to him.

"Quite an auction," said Brooke, in a friendly tone.

"Sure was, but that boat was worth every penny, I'd say old Vanderbilt got himself a real bargain there."

Brooke took out one of his hand rolled cigarettes and lit it.

"Are you from the press?" the auctioneer asked.

"Good God no! I'm here on vacation, it's my first trip to New York," he held out his hand, "Harry Brooke."

"English?"

"Yes, originally."

The auctioneer shook his hand: "Andrew Cruickshank."

"That's definitely not English!"

Cruickshank smiled. "No, Scottish originally. I came over with my parents, ten years ago now."

"Do you like it here?"

"It's very different to Glasgow, or what I remember of it. New York is very … cosmopolitan?"

"Yes, I believe it is," said Brooke light-heartedly, "I arrived a few days ago. The other passengers were from all corners of Europe, rather extraordinary. So I'm just starting to meet a few people. In fact, I met Mr Appleby earlier, and …"

"The vendor? Yeah, I feel kind of sorry for him having to part with that yacht, his pride and joy."

"Why is he parting with it?" asked Brooke, as casually as he could.

"Are you sure you're not from the press?"

"Quite sure," he replied with a smile.

"He needs the money I guess. The word is, he's being squeezed."

"Squeezed?" asked Brooke.

"Yeah, out of the shipping business."

Brooke called the bartender over and ordered a beer: "Will you join me?"

Cruickshank drained his glass, nodded approvingly: "You don't need to ask a Scotsman twice if he'd like a drink."

The barman duly delivered two large glasses of foaming beer.

"You said you'd met Mr Appleby?" said Cruickshank sipping enthusiastically at his beer, "thirsty business."

"Yes, very briefly. He introduced me to his friend."

"Friend?" responded Cruickshank, somewhat mystified.

"The man who was with him here today; you addressed him during the auction. Well, I think it was more of a jest, really."

"Friend? He's hardly a friend to Appleby."

"Really?" said Brooke.

"He's the one who's squeezing him. Daniel Crown is a very tough cookie; they say he's the most ruthless businessman in New York … and that's saying something!"

A fair-haired woman joined them, she nodded at Brooke: "You promised me lunch, Andrew. I have a good memory and an empty stomach."

He took out a pocket watch, prompting Brooke to do the same: "Oh yes, Greta this is …"

"Harry Brooke," said Brooke charmingly, "and please don't let me detain you."

Cruickshank drained his glass and put out his hand: "I'll return the compliment next time, Mr Brooke, if you are in this area."

"Thank you. Tell me, where could I find this Daniel Crown?"

Cruickshank emitted a little snigger. "I'd be very wary if I were you. The brothers have offices here on Wall Street. I couldn't tell you the number, further down, towards the water, I think. But you can't miss it, there's a plaque on the door CROWN BROTHERS. They might not be open now, if you're planning a social call."

"It being lunchtime, Mr Brooke," said Greta Cruickshank flashing an adorable smile. With that the Cruickshanks turned tail and walked away.

Brooke walked out onto Wall Street, into the bright sunlight. There was an intense reflective glare from the stonework of the buildings. It was hot, rather than warm, and he decided he would sit out the noonday heat in his hotel. The streets were busy: carriages, horse-drawn heavy haulage, and pedestrians of all sorts -

those going about their business and those immigrants who were first-footing their new homeland.

Brooke had slept off his lunch and the worst of the heat before he ventured back out of the hotel.

"Mr Le Maitre!" a voice called out from behind.

Brooke seemed oblivious.

"Mr Le Maitre! Wait up!"

Brooke then turned to see the angular features of William Appleby, sheltered by a wide-brimmed hat. Brooke had actually forgotten the improvised name he'd used a while earlier. There was no sign of Appleby's corpulent former companion.

"Yes," said Brooke in reply, his eyes squinting somewhat in the sunshine.

"Appleby, we met earlier, back at the auction, you recall?"

"But of course, yes, I'm sorry," said Brooke.

"Are you from the newspapers?" asked Appleby.

There was a swarm of people around them, Brooke spotted a sidewalk shop's awning, and indicated that they should head towards it to benefit from the shade it offered. Appleby followed Brooke's lead.

"Now you're the second person to ask me that very same question today," replied Brooke with something of a smile.

"Well, are you?"

"No, not really, not nowadays anyway, although I once acted as war correspondent for the Illustrated London News," Brooke improvised, "why do you ask?"

He was thinking: take care with improvisation, he'd nearly revealed that a colleague was a war artist.

"You are English, right?"

"Yes."

"And we haven't met before today, have we?"

"No." Better, at least, to confess this.

"So, what were you doing at the auction?"

"Killing some time before lunch - a morning's frivolous entertainment."

Appleby had noticed the auction catalogue tucked under Brooke's arm, it had cost the price of the entrance fee. Their eyes met, Appleby knew Brooke was lying.

"And your conversation with our esteemed auctioneer, Cruickshank?"

Brooke said nothing.

Appleby's thin lips twisted into a smile: "That would have been until Cruickshank's beautiful wife, Greta, arrived to sweep him away."

"So, you've been watching me?" Brooke asked, fascinated by this switch.

"Yes."

"Why?"

"Simply because I hadn't seen you before and I'd assumed you were press. And most probably you were trying to find yourself a nice juicy story, or tidbits. The New York Times just lost their society hack in a railroad accident in Rochester ... Theodore Boyle, he was a friend."

Again, Brooke said nothing.

"The cream of New York society was in that auction room, probably the entire wealth of Manhattan under one roof."

"To see the sale of a yacht?" Brooke was more intent on wiping the sweat from his face, his comment had been almost dismissive.

"No, not any yacht Mr Le Maitre, it was my yacht that was being sold - you saw it - taken from me, right before your eyes."

Appleby paused for a moment, surveying Brooke, before continuing, "So, if you're not a writer and you're not a yachtsman, what are you?"

Brooke lowered his voice: "Let's just say that I'm an interested party and leave it at that."

Brooke walked away, without further word.

Appleby watched, perplexed, as Brooke melted away into the pavement throng.

Brooke strolled along Wall Street, eventually he stood by one of the wharves, collecting his thoughts once again. He found a bench, took out his silver cigarette case, selected a cigarette and lit it. It was now late afternoon; the air was still and bordering on being oppressive - activity along these wharves didn't seem to relent. He watched the antics of a pair of gulls as returning thoughts of recent experiences in Britain tormented him. He couldn't afford to dwell on such thoughts of loss ... or love.

Brooke was ready to make his way back towards his hotel. The range of shops he passed, the commodities and services they offered was mesmerising. Broadway had been dusty, kicked up by a significant amount of horse-drawn traffic, Brooke was pleased to arrive at the hotel and step inside.

Was it his imagination, or did the bellboy cast him a furtive look as he entered the lobby?

He made his way up the two flights of stairs to his room, unlocked the door and stepped inside. Immediately, he sensed there had been an intruder and it wasn't the chambermaid; the bed covers had not been turned down yet. No, the room had been searched - his trunk, which he'd placed on a wooden luggage rack, was a little askew. He opened the trunk to find the arrangement of its contents in a slightly different order. He checked further. His old army document wallet containing correspondence and all of his travel papers had been looked through. Damn it, he thought to himself, it would have revealed his real name. The clothes in his wardrobe had also been disturbed. He cursed silently. So, who was the culprit? Appleby or Crown? He had not told anybody where he was staying, but it wouldn't be so difficult for a reasonably skilled adversary to track him down, and he'd probably attracted one since his arrival.

Brooke left the room, locking the door, went back along the corridor making his way to the staircase. He cast his eye about in search of the bellboy. Brooke found him by the water fountain and went on the offensive.

"Excuse me." he said casually and in one very swift and fluid move, took the youth's right wrist, twisting it into a painful arm lock. The boy winced with the sudden pain.

"I seem to have been burgled."

"B... b... burgled?" said the bellboy in a squeaky voice that could have originated in some European country.

Brooke produced his key in his free hand: "You see, I have my key here and yet my room has been entered. How could that be?"

Brooke increased the pressure of the arm lock; the young man winced; "I. I... Don't …"

"Oh, but you do and it's really very simple, you see. I will break your arm if you do not tell me the truth. The damage to the tendons and nerves will result in a greater agony than the break itself. You had best believe me, for I have done this on many occasions before."

The youth was breathing heavily, and tears of pain appeared in his eyes: "A guy paid me a dollar to borrow the pass key."

"How did he know which room?"

Silence. This only served to stoke Brooke's anger. Another fraction, the ulna and the radius would snap - the boy was racked with fear.

"Did he know my name?"

"N... no, he... he just asked about a big Englishman, new in town. I figured it had to be you."

"What did he look like?"

The bellboy described Appleby accurately, Brooke released the pressure of his grip, slightly.

"Do you know him?"

"No... no, sir. I surely don't ... he's a stranger."

"If he comes back, I want you to tell me, do you understand?"

The boy nodded, still quaking with fear.

"There's five dollars, if you play straight with me."

The boy nodded.

"Good. Because if you don't, the owner of this hotel, Mr Monnot, will hear that you aided and abetted a crime."

"Y... yes."

"Good," said Brooke and released his grip.

The youth slumped against the water fountain exhausted, holding his wrist, crying with relief.

Crown Brothers' premises were located at the bottom end of Wall Street between a book store and a realtor. As described by the auctioneer, a name plaque on the front door confirmed the name, but not the nature of the business. Brooke knocked on the door, hard, but there was no response. The sun was less intense now, it would have been the close of business for most offices. As Brooke made his way further down Wall Street, he found a service alley running parallel behind the street. It was filled with the refuse and detritus of the many foodstuff traders. Brooke walked back, counting thirty rear entrances, in order to find Crown Brothers. There was a set of stairs up to a second floor and a substantial-looking door. He took out Bishop's treasured set of skeleton keys, cautiously trying each one. These blanks, as they were known, had been made and supplied to Bishop by a sympathetic English locksmith ... and, CLICK, he felt one slot into place.

Brooke looked over his shoulder quickly, left and right, nobody in sight. All seemed quiet, now it was Brooke's turn to be the intruder.

The offices on the second level were commodious, with

expensive furnishings and fittings. Shafts of sunlight shone through the blinds, illuminating the rooms in almost theatrical fashion. On one door he noticed a sign: WOLFSOHN & BACHARAH, Attorneys at Law. On another: DANIEL CROWN - Banking and Finance. They seemed to be the same company, but with different names. Who were these people? Brooke opened the door, as if creeping into some inner sanctuary. The desk was strewn with documents; his attention was drawn to a banker's draft; COOPER WATTS AUCTIONEERS made out to Mr William Appleby for $6,900. A quick calculation suggested six thousand dollars, plus fifteen per cent buyer's commission. He picked it up and examined it very closely. Obviously, this was payment for the sale of the yacht, but what was it doing here? Were Crown and Appleby working together after all ? Was Cruickshank wrong in his estimation of their relationship?

On an easel was a list of dates and names, which seemed to outline the history of the transatlantic steamship business. There was an artist's impression of the SS Great Britain's maiden voyage to New York in 1843. There were also some similar sketches of Cunard's vessels. But most important, it would seem, was a company profile.

Company Registration

TRADING NAME: The Appleby Mail and Steamship Company.
BUSINESS: Maritime, mercantile trading and transportation.
FATE: Bankruptcy, following a total loss at sea and subsequent termination of Government subsidy.
FOUNDED: 1832.
SHAREHOLDERS: Edward (deceased), Thomas, William and Victoria Appleby.
DEFUNCT: 1852.
BUSINESS BASE: New York.
SERVING: Transatlantic and Gulf of Mexico routes.

PRINCIPALS: Appleby shareholders; Daniel Crown.
SHIPS: SS Cincinnati (x), SS Indianapolis, SS St. Louis, SS Baltimore.
COMPETITORS: Cunard Line.
GOV'T. CONTRACTS: Mail; occasional military.
GOV'T. SUBSIDIES: $385,000 per annum, occasionally more (terminated 1852).
CROWN SHAREHOLDING: $300,000 (25%).

Brooke absorbed as much as he could; he wasn't a businessman, but the profile gave him a fairly clear impression. He riffled through the papers carefully, then spotted something he could not have possibly anticipated, it was a drawing of the deep-water pier at Portbury and the Great Western Railway spur from Bristol, the very thing that Arbuthnott and Brunel had hired him to investigate originally.

What the hell was this doing here? Brooke thought that had all ended at Newton Meadows. At the foot of the detailed drawing, someone had written a note:

Daniel - this concept must be eradicated at all costs - I suggest we/you force the scheme and company into insolvency.

There was a sound beneath, downstairs a door was opening, he heard the sounds of voices and of laughter. Brooke swallowed hard, every nerve in his body now alert. There was a creak of the first step on the wooden staircase from the Wall Street entrance to the building. Brooke dropped the drawing back on the desk, not having time to replace it accurately.

"SOMEONE THERE?" a voice shouted loudly, "Mrs. Moore, is that you? HELL!" the voice sounded a little slurred. There was more than one person. Brooke sped for the back door, opened it, stepped outside, closing it behind him. Now, which of the blank keys was it? He swiftly sorted through the blanks and locked the door. On the other side, Brooke could hear banging and the raised voice: "WHO THE HELL IS THIS?"

The voice sounded both drunk and angry.

Brooke scrambled down the rear steps to the service alley. He tumbled against a wall, caught his breath and hastened his stride towards the river. As he turned the corner at the end of the block, a familiar face greeted him.

"Surprised, Mr Brooke?" said Appleby, the thin lips twisted into a smile. Inside Appleby's coat Brooke could clearly see he was carrying a holstered revolver. Confronting an armed opponent is never easy, but Brooke calculated that if it were an American revolver, as he'd previously experienced, it would not be cocked whilst holstered. Brooke executed a fast kick to Appleby's right calf and was about to follow this up with a blow from his elbow.

Appleby collapsed and screamed, "STOP IT! CAN'T YOU SEE WE'RE ON THE SAME SIDE?"

Brooke hesitated; was this some kind of trick?

"Look behind you!" Appleby gasped.

Sure enough, at the top of the fire escape he saw two of Crown's men. They began to descend, and their weapons were not holstered.

Appleby was intent on escape: "Come on, Brooke. Follow me. Quickly!"

They scurried around the corner onto Wall Street, where a horse and carriage were waiting.

"GO. GO. GO!" Appleby shouted at the driver, who immediately followed his instruction. Brooke and Appleby were running alongside the carriage as it gained momentum. They clambered aboard as two shots rang out over their heads.

Appleby struggled with the door, Brooke dived in.

A third shot caught Appleby somewhere in the lower leg: "DAMN!" he screamed and fell into the carriage. The wound started to bleed badly.

Brooke found himself on his knees as Appleby fussed in attempt to unholster his weapon, too late to see off Crown's men - they were now out of range and there were too many passers-by in between.

"Crown wouldn't risk any injury to members of the public … we're all right … for the moment." He leaned out of the window, calling to the driver, "Well executed, Mr Powell, I guess you're hired! Take us to ninety-eight, East Twenty-Eighth Street, and hurry!"

20 EAST 28TH STREET, NEW YORK CITY

3rd June 1852

"How's the leg?" asked Brooke, clutching a large tumbler of whisky.

A young lady was tending to Appleby's wound with various solutions and dressings. She seemed to know what she was doing, Brooke watched her with some interest.

"He'll live," she said, in a voice without a trace of an immigrant accent. She finished up, but not before replenishing both of their glasses. She then left.

"What were you doing in Crown's office? It obviously wasn't a social call ... he's not known for shooting clients, or guests leaving by the rear exit ... not during the daytime anyways."

They were above an art gallery in an elegantly-appointed salon, befitting a lady's tastes. Perhaps it did belong to a lady.

Brooke finished his drink and fixed Appleby with a stare.

"I might ask what you were doing searching my hotel room."

"Who said it was me?" replied Appleby, absent-mindedly caressing his bandaged leg, "Ouch! This is sore!"

Now it was Brooke's turn to replenish the glasses.

"I did," said Brooke, "and don't fiddle with the wound, if you want it to heal."

Appleby smiled, "I wanted to find out who you were - since you obviously were not Phillip Le Maitre - good name, by the way."

"Spur of the moment choice," Brooke raised his glass accepting the compliment, "go on, you have my attention."

"I followed you - with two others - to your hotel and then back to Wall Street. You went to the address that Andrew Cruickshank had given you."

Brooke sipped the whisky: "And what makes you think we're on the same side?"

"You weren't at Cooper Watts to buy a gaff schooner, and, as we have now established, you are not a writer for the New York Times. You are a man who arrived in this city, aboard the SS Great Britain from England a short time ago - and yes, I did see your ticket - but I had already checked through the ship's manifest. First class cabin and a very enviable bar bill!"

Brooke said nothing.

"I'd say you are a private investigator of some sort, and by the speed at which you floored me earlier on, I would imagine you are a former military man. How am I doing so far?"

Brooke wandered towards the window: "Why was there a cheque made out to you, for the proceeds from the sale of your yacht, on Daniel Crown's desk?"

"Good question," said Appleby.

"Well, I'm listening."

"This is about war, Mr Brooke. As a soldier, you will understand that concept," he waited to see if Brooke would deny his military background.

Brooke said nothing.

"As Senator Seward said to Congress in a patriotic response to the perceived British maritime threat from Cunard: 'The contest is for the ultimate empire of the ocean, the struggle for the freedom of commerce of the seas.' You see, for a man like Seward this was tantamount to war, a conflict being forced upon the United States by Great Britain, through Cunard's ambition to control the

Atlantic. 'The field of battle' he said, 'is chosen, not by us, but by the enemy, it is not a provincial contest for provincial objects, but a national one. We must meet our adversary on that field, not elsewhere, and we must meet him or surrender the whole nation's cause without a blow.'"

"Strong words," said Brooke, taking a cigarette out his silver case and lighting it.

"Heartfelt words, Mr Brooke. The feeling was, why should we pander once again to British interests following everything that had been achieved after the War of 1812? Our prospering nationhood, transatlantic routes, mail, concerns about anti-American feeling and antipathy towards the country. These were common sentiments from the floor of the House of Representatives."

As if thinking aloud, "Hence the Lafayette connection?" Brooke mused, to test the water.

Appleby looked surprised by this comment, his response being, "HELL NO! WELL, YES AND NO! That was a patriotic family obsession against the British, handed down through a couple of generations. And my estranged cousin Thomas in England, he's another fanatical fantasist!"

Brooke said nothing.

"Cunard was already receiving a very substantial subsidy from the British Government, the Admiralty in fact, and additional finance from ... guess who?"

"Daniel Crown?"

"Exactly! A double-dealing player, except we didn't know that at the time, of course. The dice were loaded, and so ..." Appleby sipped his drink and looked at Brooke; it was a pause, a calculation on how much he should reveal, but in fact, he had nothing to lose. "My brother and I secured an annual mail subsidy for the Appleby Steamship Line: three hundred and eighty-five thousand dollars from the US Government - a tidy sum - and we approached Daniel Crown to participate in financing the venture."

"Which he did?" interjected Brooke, thinking back to the company profile he'd seen in Crown's offices.

"Which he did, yes. Crown put up three hundred thousand dollars, buying in to the company and giving himself a twenty-five percent share. He became the largest stakeholder in the venture. But as I said, the Crown family and its associates were backing Cunard too, thus giving them a dominating and controlling interest in the North Atlantic mail and steam packets - indirectly, they were receiving large subsidies from both governments."

"Very shrewd on their part, though?"

Appleby took another pause, sipping at his whisky.

"Daniel Crown convinced us to form a secret cartel with Cunard, a 'syndicate' as he called it, to keep out any competition. This arrangement set minimum fares for passengers, controlled cargo charges and of course the mail - all with a guaranteed split of the revenues; two thirds to Cunard and one third to us."

"Wasn't that illegal?" suggested Brooke.

"Yes but hidden within plain sight of the authorities; and because of the often precarious state of relations between Britain and America, it was in everyone's interest to maintain the status quo. The American public and its vociferous press - of which I thought you were one - expected us to destroy Cunard, not to establish a cosy relationship with our supposed prime rival."

"A complicated web?" said Brooke, recalling one of Bishop's favoured descriptions.

"Yes. And then we received word of Mr Brunel's audacious plan and knew that had to be stopped. We had thought he was finished as a global competitor, and indeed he was in terms of a steamship line offering a regular service between Britain and America."

"But what was the reasoning?"

"Simple. Position and fuel consumption; Brunel was right. Bristol to New York by sail and steam would have been less expensive and faster. Neither Cunard nor Appleby ships were as economic as Brunel's designs, but both companies and Crown had vested interests in Liverpool. Brunel's route was straight and much shorter. But in the end, it didn't matter."

"Why so?"

Appleby rose rather awkwardly and fetched the bottle of whisky from the drinks cabinet, holding it up in Brooke's direction.

"Yes … thank you … that's fine."

Appleby sat and put his hands together, as if in prayer. "Last winter, disaster struck. The SS Cincinnati sailed from Liverpool with more than two hundred and sixty passengers and crew, including my brother, my wife and our daughter."

"What happened?"

"The ship encountered fog between Cape Farewell, Greenland

and St. John, Newfoundland. She was hundreds of miles off course. We think she may have either collided with an iceberg or struck a wreck, who knows? The ship took on water ... the ship's captain would have tried to reach land, but a hundred miles from Nova Scotia, she apparently rolled over and sank. She'd been spotted by fishing vessels, but they were unable to offer assistance." He sniffed, visibly moved by recounting the tragedy.

"My God, I am sorry, Mr Appleby."

"Not one survivor, she sank without trace."

Appleby drained his glass: "Within three months, the public had lost confidence. A short time after that, the Appleby Line lost the U.S. Government subsidy. We were ruined."

"And Crown?"

"He still held all the aces. He diverted his interest to Cunard, who were still receiving the subsidies, and were also benefiting from the fact that the threat from Brunel and his Bristol scheme had vanished."

"And you were saddled with the debts of a failed business, hence why you have had to sell the yacht; yes I can see all of this now ... but what about your other ships?"

"I expect Crown will sell them for scrap, to cover his costs and our debt; those ships have been tainted, as is our family name."

"I suppose the ship-owning fraternity is a small community with key players and is susceptible to the prejudices of the general public."

Appleby could only nod, he was exhausted.

"But if you could prove Crown acted illegally ..." said Brooke, although he already knew the answer to this.

"What good would that do? I acted illegally too, my late brother and I were both culpable."

"And then there is the question of Thomas Appleby, your estranged cousin in England." Brooke arched an eyebrow as he considered how he was going to deliver further bad news.

Appleby turned to face Brooke, his features had lost expression, he was drained of colour, "What of him?"

"He's dead - I was the one who shot him. It was in self-defence, at Newton Meadows House."

"I suppose I should be angry, or vengeful, but for some reason, I am not," he said after a few moments contemplation. And what of his sister Victoria? Did you see her?"

"I believe that in the end, she took her own life. That is really all I know," Brooke lied.

"I see, Mr Brooke, that's it then … well now we both know the truth, don't we? So, what will you do next?"

"Go home: the SS Great Britain leaves for Liverpool on the 5th of June."

"And then?" enquired Appleby, with the vaguest hint of a smile, for he knew that Brooke would not tell him, but it was worth asking anyway.

21 THE DOLPHIN HOTEL, LIVERPOOL

20th August 1852

Harry Brooke walked out of the Dolphin Hotel, where he had taken rooms for a month, and looked out across the Mersey. It was a warm day and he was in a contemplative mood. He had an important meeting at noon which would settle the direction of his future life. He took out his silver cigarette case, lit one of his hand-rolled cigarettes and looked at the SS Great Britain. She'd had a thorough refit the previous year after it was decided to create a new service to Melbourne; the recent discovery of gold at Ballarat had transformed Australia from a place of exile to a land of opportunity.

William Patterson had been commissioned to change the vessel from a sail-assisted steamship to a steam-assisted sailing ship. The 12,000-mile voyage was now within reach, and the excitement was all over Liverpool. There was now a new dining saloon in the deckhouse, with a partition separating Fore- and After-Saloon passengers. The Ladies' Drawing Room with its large windows was

147

now in the stern, and extensive carpeting had been fitted to reduce rattle and engine noise. Further forward were the sleeping quarters and mess rooms for the officers and crew; the doctor's surgery, barber's shop, steward's pantry, bar, bakehouse, three galleys and carpenters' and joiners' workshops. The formerly resplendent dining saloon had been converted to steerage accommodation and was also being used as an extended cargo hold. This, together with the compactness of the new engines and boilers, meant that cargo capacity had increased to nearly 1000 tonnes. To boost shipboard rations, live animals were carried to serve as a mobile farm. It was an extraordinary feat of imagination and hard work. She was due to sale tomorrow, 21st August 1852, and all was looking good.

Brooke, however, was in a bind from which he could not escape, despite an offer of a new job, which Brunel undoubtedly had a hand in. His spirits were so low because, in the time he had been back from New York, he had been unable to return to Bristol; Brunel's instructions had been clear. Brooke could not afford to be recognised, which in maritime circles, he surely would be. And yet he longed to see his beloved Isabelle. Thoughts of her pervaded his mind as each day passed, and he could not shift them. Had she passed her music exam and returned to Paris?

He was disinclined to travel down to Richmond Hill to see Cornelius Arbuthnott, and even less inclined to visit Lincoln's Inn Fields and the ghost of Miss Appleby. He still needed to file a report on his mission to New York. In those few weeks, he had achieved a great deal. After his return to Liverpool Brooke had trekked through the Peak District with a guide from Buxton to relax and kill time whilst not on duty, but deciding what he should write in his report had consumed his mind. How much should he reveal? He was not a literary man; he was a soldier and a man of action.

My Dear Cornelius. Dear Mr Arbuthnott ... how should he even commence such an account? More importantly, who would its readers be? In whose interest would it be to discover the truth and the real identity of the dark forces described in the first place? Arbuthnott and Blackfriars certainly; Isambard, most definitely. Even the Prime Minister, Edward Smith-Stanley, for whom Arbuthnott ultimately worked, may want to know whether there was a political angle. Not to mention Parliament and the Admiralty. And yet, Isambard had funded him, had he not? The GWR envelope at the Royal Western in Bristol ...

Brooke cleared his throat, looked to his left and right to ensure he was not overheard and whispered the following words to himself: 'Gentlemen, as you are all aware, I have recently visited America, as an independent investigator with a question: why had the Great Western Steam Company, which opened steam communications with America, not had the opportunity to gain the mail contract?'

He sighed; yes, it was a start.

Barnard Robert Matthews had been appointed as the new Captain of the SS Great Britain. He was an experienced sailor, having commanded sailing ships on many transatlantic voyages following the emigration boom after the Great Famine in Ireland. Although he possessed many social graces, he had also been described as crusty and disagreeable. Brooke got on well with him and understood his ways; he'd had many encounters with such people before. After the ship's return from New York, Captain Martin, the company's Marine Superintendent, had asked John Gray to join the ship's complement as a Second Officer. Brooke was scheduled to meet the Captain shortly to discuss his own role.

Tomorrow the SS Great Britain would carry 630 passengers (the most she could carry on the Australia route), a crew of 138, and a full cargo which included gold and silver specie (coins) valued at £1 million. Many of the passengers had all their worldly goods either stowed in the hold or in their cabins: all their jewellery and their life savings. With such riches aboard, she was equipped to resist attack. Six 8-pounder guns were mounted on deck, and she carried arms and ammunition for 100 men, including muskets and pikes to repel boarders or pirates. It was predicted the voyage would take 56 days. This time the company had secured the valuable Royal Mail contracts, and in its eagerness to obtain them, it had guaranteed delivery within 60 days. The ship bunkered with 1400 tons of coal, which was considered enough for the entire passage. But, it was decided, wisely as it turned out, to take on fresh supplies at Cape Town, and colliers were sent ahead. In short, the SS Great Britain was a floating treasure trove and what they needed was an experienced, trusted Marshall. Possibly with military experience and enthusiastic references.

Brooke checked his pocket watch as Captain Matthews approached the Dolphin Hotel's entrance. Twelve o'clock exactly;

he was punctual. Brooke held out his hand as the man approached.

Tomorrow history would be made, and they would both be part of it.

EPILOGUE

The SS Great Britain, 24th August 1852

The matronly lady sitting on the weather deck with Harry Brooke wraps her cloak around herself. It is getting cold. Brooke notices that it is in fact a man's cloak, large, with a clasp at its neck. There is a small engraving on it – Primum non nocere – Greek. 'First do no harm.' The words don't strike him as having any significance, yet.

"My goodness Mr Brooke," she says, quite fascinated, "but tell me, what happened after the conversation you had with Mr Appleby? East 28th Street, New York City, as I recall?"

Brooke gazes out to sea and sighs: "Well, I considered my assignment was over. So, I returned to my hotel."

"And? I sense there is a bit more to this story."

"When I arrived at my room, they were waiting for me. Three of them, including Mr Daniel Crown himself. Initially he became quite aggressive, asking questions and demanding answers. One of his men grabbed hold of my coat lapel. I don't approve of people grabbing my clothes like that, and so, I warned him. He laughed and threw a few punches. I'd roasted lesser men in the foothills of Afghanistan, so it got a bit rough. But Mr Crown didn't want to ruin his suit either." Brooke goes on to say that he had quickly rendered two of Crown's thugs unconscious, leaving him and Crown to talk alone. The lady, though shocked, was not surprised. She senses Brooke is not a man to be crossed or doubted. But she has other reasons too. He continues, "I persuaded Mr Crown to buy the yacht back from Vanderbilt – at a slightly inflated price - and give it to Mr Appleby. I am sure it would have caused quite a stir in those New York financial circles."

"Because you reasoned, and quite rightly so, that he deserved it; it was his pride and joy after all. It was sheer spite on Crown's part. He didn't need the money."

"I'm traditional in matters like that, you see," Brooke says with a self-deprecating smile.

The lady shivers, "What manner of threat could you have issued to persuade him to do such a thing?"

Brooke chuckles: "I didn't mention to you that I lifted a single piece of paper from Crown's office desk, the day I gained access."

"Broke in, to be more precise."

"Yes."

"Which was, what?"

"Do you remember the banker's draft from Cooper Watts Auctioneers made out to Appleby for $6,900?"

"Of course I do."

Brooke looks her in the eye: "Crown had a choice. Either he bought the yacht back from Vanderbilt; or the legitimate investors in Britain and America would hear of his double dealing. Let alone US Congress and the Admiralty. In short, I threatened him."

She shakes her head: "Blackmailing a man like that?"

"If that's the word you chose to use, then yes. I make no excuse."

"I wasn't being judgmental," she says with a slight edge.

Brook sits forward, thinking they should soon go below as it's getting dark. "If you think about it, whatever he had to pay Vanderbilt was small fish to keep his financial and commercial reputation intact; and himself out of prison. And of course, Appleby received the cheque as well."

The lady laughs out loud: "Crown must have been furious!"

"Spitting blood was the expression I heard from someone on the homeward voyage back to Liverpool! And yes, he deserved it." There are a few moments of silence while they both digest what has taken place between them: a conversation between two strangers and a confession from Harry Brooke; but there is more. Brooke stands and stretches: "There was also the vaguely implied suggestion that Crown may have taken advantage of the SS Cincinnati tragedy by dumping the Appleby Mail Steamship Company and switching all of his energies to Cunard – rather than supporting it at its time of need."

The lady also stands: "He would rather his enemy capitulated than have to vanquish them?"

"Yes," says Harry, "I like that. When we arrive in Australia, I shall write a letter to Cornelius in Richmond Hill and use those very words!"

After a momentary pause, the lady casts him a glance; not suspicious, not accusing, just curious. "And what of the Lafayette necklace?" she asks, perplexed.

"In what manner?"

"What is it? What is the significance of it?"

"Ah," says Brooke, amused, "because it's really two questions, isn't it? The other being – why did the Swindon assailant have it amongst the folds of his clothes?"

"Yes, do tell."

"Gilbert du Motier – the Marquis de Lafayette. He was immensely symbolic for some of the Appleby clan. He was a noble French soldier who defeated the British in America in the 1770s. I understand he helped give the Americans freedom from British rule. We know Thomas's father died fighting for it in Virginia. The necklace belonged to Lafayette; so yes, it was very significant to the Applebys as a trophy." Brooke pauses. "As to why Charles had it – who knows? I think he stole it, from his father. And took the cyanide lest he got caught. It's in the ship's safe, by the way, in case you want to see it."

"At some stage, yes. But there are other things more pressing …" The lady suddenly releases the clasp of her cloak to reveal a nurse's uniform underneath it. Brooke is confused and then remembers a notion he considered when he first met this charming lady – first do no harm. "Mr Brooke, I fear I have not been entirely frank with you," she says mysteriously.

"You have been an admirable audience, we must have been here for hours!"

There is something in her voice now; a change in her tone and manner: "Please ... come with me, below, to the Drawing Room," she says, softly but firmly, more of a request than an invitation.

Brooke is confused: "Now? Why? What on earth are you talking about?"

She smiles at him in a way he just can't fathom. "You see, while I am currently engaged as the ship's senior nurse, I am also Mrs. Mary Hartland, my husband is ..."

"Dr Percival Hartland of the Bristol Infirmary; but of course, now I understand. That's why you said your husband is in the sick bay - as a physician - not a patient as I assumed. This is quite unbelievable."

"It is no crime to assume, Mr Brooke. But you see Percival is attending to a specific patient. Her care has absorbed so much of his time these last three days, a very bad case of the seemingly obligatory sea-sickness - poor girl. But I am pleased to say, she has now found her sea-legs and is effectively recovered - thank goodness."

Poor girl? Had he misheard something? His heart misses a beat.

"Now we may proceed below, please follow me."

First do no harm.

As they enter the Ladies' Drawing Room, Brooke becomes aware of music; the sound of a piano.

The Moonlight Sonata. Seated at the piano, Isabelle.

"My uncle promised you the moonlight, remember, Mr Brooke?"

His eyes close; his thoughts are tangled and disjointed - those scrambled dreams. The likelihood of this outcome - can this be reality?

"Mademoiselle Loiseau?"

Mary Hartland discreetly leaves.

Isabelle rises from the piano and runs into Brooke's arms.

"I don't know what to say."

"Then say nothing."

She kisses her index finger and places it upon his lips - an instruction: "Don't say a word, just hold me ... hold me close."

He wraps his arms around her, closing his eyes again.

"I know of your loss, of Peter Bishop, of the sorrow you must

154

surely feel," she is whispering, "and, since we knew that you were actually aboard the ship, I have been too ill. For everything that has happened, I am so, so sorry," she is tearful.

Brooke can sense his own tears coursing down his cheeks.

"He told you, Mr Brooke - a promise is a promise," she says softly into his ear.

"I know … 'Have faith, Harry,' he said, 'always have faith - you'll see'."

"Those words didn't let you down, did they? And neither did I."

"No," says Brooke, "it was his prophecy, a new beginning."

Vague thoughts that had given him some comfort through the recent months of secluded travel and his adventures in America, thoughts of being with her, of loving her, are now the foundations of a new life. And he can't believe his good fortune.

The End

REFERENCES

'The Ocean Railway.' Stephen Fox. Harper Collins: 2003.
'When Britain burned the White House: The 1814 Invasion of Washington.' Peter Snow. John Murray: 2013.
'Brunel.' Angus Buchanan. Continuum: 2001.
'Bristol: Maritime City.' Frank Shipsides. Redcliffe: 1981.
'Brunel.' LTC Rolt. Trinity: 1965.
'The Voyages of the Great Britain.' Nicholas Fogg. Chatham: 2002.
'The Annals of Bristol History.' John Latimer (1-9). 1863.
'Report of the Lords of the Committee of Privy Council for Trade on the Abandonment of Portbury Pier and Railway.' House of Commons: 1852.
'Portbury Pier and Railway. Plan and Section.' IK Brunel: 1845.
'Harbours and Docks.' Francis Vernon Harcourt: 1885.
'IKB through time' – John Christopher. Amberley 2010.
'Brunel – the man who built the world' – Steven Brindle. Orion 2005.
'The First Atlantic Liner' – Helen Doe. Amberley 2017.
'The Illustrated Guide to the GREAT WESTERN RAILWAY 1852' – George Measom. Countryside Books 1985. (First published 1852.)
The Brunel Archive in Bristol / Selected papers, letters and original documents.

PERMISSIONS

We are grateful to COUNTRYSIDE BOOKS of Newbury for permission to reproduce the facsimile illustrations from GWR 1852 by George Measom; to City of Westminster Archives for granting us permission to license 'Anonymous sketch, looking towards Eastbourne Terrace (Paddington, London)'; to Bristol Central Library for their permission to use the lithographs of The Royal Western Hotel, the Bristol Infirmary, Blaise Castle House and Smyth House; and to The SS Great Britain Trust for the picture of SS Great Britain.

AUTHOR'S NOTE

Stuart Amesbury and I first met some forty years ago when I moved into a flat in the large Victorian house where he lives in Bristol. By coincidence, my father had lived in the same house back in the early 1950s. My career took me away to East Anglia and abroad, but throughout the ensuing years Stuart and I remained in touch. About five years ago, we were having a drink at the Nova Scotia, a famous old Bristolian pub by the river.

'What do you know of King Road?' I asked him casually; a rhetorical question, because it is not a road, but a stretch of water along the foreshore of Portbury between Portishead and the mouth of the River Avon. The reason for asking was that I had been asked by Gerry Brooke, then the editor of the Bristol Times newspaper, to write a piece on Isambard Kingdom Brunel which featured his association with Bristol, particularly with places and his historical landmarks. I had previously written a few short stories for the paper; the novelty being to blend fact and fiction to tell a story.

The story Gerry outlined should start at Paddington Station and follow the GWR track down through Swindon, Box, Bath and finally Temple Meads (or Bristol Terminus); all Brunel landmarks. He wanted about 2,000 words and a few illustrations to depict Brunel's brilliance as a visionary engineer. In fact, I decided to call the piece 'Brunel's Vision.' And for good reason. I reached 2,500 words and had only just reached the Box Tunnel. I discovered the fact that the sun shines through the eastern portal of the tunnel at dawn on April 9th, Brunel's birthday; a phenomenon which perplexed engineers for decades: how did he do it?

'Too many words,' said Gerry, and the newspaper story was shelved. I had become fascinated by Brunel's vision of a seamless journey from London via Bristol to New York on one single ticket. The concept was unheard of; in fact, Bristol and London existed in two different time zones. Brunel's vision was an example of his genius and originality.

Except, it didn't happen. Although a company was formed to create this transatlantic route, it was abandoned in 1852. The question remained: why? It made no sense. Stuart's research began in earnest. Finally he uncovered a vital piece of evidence which explained the significance and importance of the scheme, but not the reason why it hadn't been carried through, so we dug deeper.

It was then that we decided to turn the project into a work of semi-fiction, retaining the factual background. We invented fictional characters to share their lives with real people. The idea developed into an audio drama: 'Brunel's Vision – One Single Ticket'. It was produced by the University of the West of England (UWE) and performed by a cast of actors. The soundtrack is awash with Victorian sound effects. The final recording was produced as a CD and digital download, and the project launched at the Clifton Suspension Bridge on 1st December 2017 as a tribute to Mr Brunel. The event was opened by the Lord Mayor and attended by a hundred guests; local publicity was very enthusiastic.

We had enough material for a novel. It should open and close on board the SS Great Britain on her inaugural voyage to Australia in August 1852. Harry Brooke – the hero – relates his story to a stranger, a lady who becomes crucial to his future. The result is ONE SINGLE TICKET; edited by Nicky Coates and designed beautifully by Leonard & Bryony Greenwood. The novel is illustrated with lithographs to complement the narrative.

Robert Wallace, 2019
www.rob-wallace.co.uk
www.onesingleticket.co.uk
www.brunelsvision.co.uk

The reason why Brunel's floating pier and harbour at Portbury were abandoned remains another Bristol Mystery.

Printed in Great Britain
by Amazon